Bloody Red Nose

Fifteen Fears of a Clown

Bloody Red Nose

Fifteen Fears of a Clown

Edited by
Dave Higgins

And featuring stories by
Willow Croft
Eleanor Cawood Jones
Ben Fitts
Casey Douglass
Simon Petersen
Jeremy Megargee
Robert Morgan Fisher
Ray Kolb
Misha Burnett
Dan Allen
M. Kelly Peach
Gord Sellar
Andreas Hort
Kathleen Palm
Daniel Scott White

Contents

Introduction

I don't know whether clowns have always been objects of fear. What I do know is that I wasn't scared of them when I was young. One of my father's colleagues had a sideline as a party clown, so my parent's booked him for— I think—my fifth birthday party. I remember being so excited when I saw him getting out of his car that I ran out of the house. And my best friend loved him so much, his parents booked the same clown to do his party a couple of months later. I discovered while editing this anthology that he's still clowning.

Decades later, I'm still not scared of clowns; but I am aware of John Wayne Gacy and other children's entertainers who used the make-up and buffoonery to camouflage their cruelty; and of the rash of scary clown sightings.

The idea for this anthology grew from that tension between entertainer and monster.

At the start of the year, Misha Burnett challenged several short-story writers (myself included) to publish an anthology this year. As the first book I'd published was an anthology, I immediately accepted the challenge. It's therefore fitting one of his short stories appears in it.

To "help" anyone who wasn't sure of a theme for their anthology, he also shared a humorous genre generator. My result was "horror noir clowns on the run".

I chuckled at the image and moved on. But, by the time I'd finished supper, I had two good ideas for short stories that fitted; and if I could come up with two interesting ideas in less than a day, other people were bound to find even more spins on it. It no longer seemed quite such a crazy theme.

So, the next day, I drafted a call for submissions and waited to see if I'd get enough to fill a book.

What I received were enough stories to fill several books over.

So, one anthology became two: this one, filled with stories of human threats; and its companion, filled with tales of the paranormal and fantastical.

With the clown such a powerful image of villain in the media, perhaps we forget that, for every serial killer or paedophile who dresses up as a clown, there are hundreds of clowns who are ordinary people not monsters.

These fifteen tales are about clowns who aren't the bad guy: clowns facing prejudice; clowns facing fear; clowns hiding from criminals.

These are the fears of a clown.

—Dave Higgins, 23rd July 2019

A Bad Day for a Clown

Willow Croft

He froze. It was coming for him. Lunging, mouth foaming. *Don't run*, he remembered, *don't show fear.*

"Winston," a voice yelled. It stopped its assault, still barking. "Winston," the voice chastised. The beast dropped its head, whined, tail drooping as it headed back to its owner. "I am so sorry. He's usually not like this. Let me put him in the house, and I'll show you where to set up. You need some space for the balloon station, correct? Be right back."

He nodded, feeling the sweat drip down the back of his costume.

"That was a close one. I'm guessing you don't have a dog, do you?"

A kindly voice, this time. Brown hair, short, a little older. With a kind face to match the voice.

"No, I don't. Not since I was a kid. About their age, I guess." He pointed at the sugared-up children running around, screaming and laughing.

"I'm Martine." She held out her hand.

He tried to shake her hand but it was hard with his big white glove. "Albert."

"Albert. Fitting name for a clown."

He couldn't tell if that was a compliment. It felt like forever since he said more than a few words to a woman. *When?* Maybe a couple of awkward dates after his divorce.

"How long?"

"Excuse me?" His makeup hid his blush.

"How long have you been a clown?"

"Oh–"

"Albert." The dog owner was waving him over from the deck.

Martine pressed into his side. He felt her breath against his ear. "Maybe we can continue this conversation, say, over dinner? Call me."

He turned back, but she was gone. In his hand was a scribbled phone number. He smiled. He felt the white face paint crack a little. *Not that one, your clown smile.*

His ears rang as he walked down the street to the bus stop. *Getting too old for this.* A thud hit the chain-link fence to his right as he passed. It was worse when you couldn't see them. Just scuffling and growling behind the fence covered with ivy. Each yard he passed greeted him with more barking, until there was an entire orchestra of dogs joining in the evening performance. He saw the bus pull up ahead of him, his shining and safe haven against the dark.

He tried not to sleep on the bus. Twenty minutes later, he was trudging up the front walk to his house. First one pocket, then the other. No keys. Not in his bag. Nowhere. *Damn it.* His hands were aching so badly he didn't even care if someone stole his clown kit. Around the back to retrieve the key underneath the flower pot, back to the front, and into his house. The silence pressed up against him. Empty. Martine's kind face.

He locked the door behind him, and went over to his phone. Dialed the number he'd already memorized. Ringing. *Don't hang up, leave a message.* But she picked up on the third ring.

"Martine?"

"Albert, how nice to hear from you so soon."

She really was kind. "Uh. Would you like to have dinner tomorrow night?"

"Tomorrow night would be lovely."

Vicino's. Eight o'clock. He barely even remembered the rest of the conversation. *Get out of your costume before you have to have it dry-cleaned.*

The next day was warm and sunny. *A good day.* There were no dogs barking at him as he went shopping. New shirt, flowers. *Did you still buy chocolates for a lady?* He jumped as something slammed into his side.

"Oh, I'm very sorry. She's such a clown. Harmless, don't worry." He looked down. A mutt was straining at her leash, wagging her tail. Not barking. Around her neck was a bandana with little clowns on it.

"Come on, Annie." The young man and the clown dog joined a bunch of other animals under a banner that said Westside Animal Shelter Adopt-a-thon.

Albert followed. Still no barking dogs among the rest of the waiting-to-be-adopted dogs. Annie looked at him with those big brown eyes, tail slapping against the pavement.

"She likes you," the young man said.

More than just a good day. A new day. Ten minutes later, Albert was filling out the adoption paperwork for Annie.

"Here's your coupon—thirty percent off for adopters inside the store here."

"Thanks, Richard," Albert smiled at the young man.

"Thank you for giving Annie a forever home."

Inside Pets N' Paws, he picked out a bed, food, toys, treats—more than he could afford, even with the coupon.

"But you're worth it, my little clown." He patted the dog on the head, and it leaned into him as they stood in line.

By the time he got home, and set up his house for his new roommate, it was almost time to get ready to leave.

He barely had time to iron his new shirt.

"How do I look," he asked Annie. The dog whined. "I'll be back soon, I promise. Be good." He kissed the dog on the head.

He arrived at Vicino's a little after eight. He looked around but didn't see her. His stomach sank. *Too good to be true.*

That breathy voice against his ear. That faint cinnamon smell.

"Sorry I'm late."

She was out of breath. Odd, she was even slightly sweaty, like she'd been running.

Don't point that out. "You look lovely," he said, instead.

"Why, thank you. These flowers are wonderful. And chocolate, too? I knew you would be a gentleman." She smiled, that kind smile, but one that hinted at something more.

Dinner passed in a wonderful haze. Delicious food, wine—he hadn't felt so good in years. He hoped she was feeling the same way.

'So, Albert—"

He felt her foot caress his leg under the table. Definitely feeling the same way.

"As you know, I'm a teacher. We have our spring carnival tomorrow, and the magician the school hired cancelled at the last minute. I wondered if you could fill in tomorrow. We can't pay you very much—"

"Of course, Martine, I'd be delighted to help out."

"Gentlemanly, and charming." She leaned over and kissed him. Not too long, a public kiss. Sweet and soft. And tasting of cinnamon.

A new day.

He'd forgotten to get another set of keys made. *Tomorrow.* He closed his eyes as Italian opera played a lullaby in his head.

Barking. Growling. Annie running around in the hall. He could hear her nails on the tile floor of the kitchen. He looked at the clock. Two a.m.

He groaned. Headed through the kitchen's connecting door to the back room. Annie was circling the back door, growling at it.

"What is it?" He rubbed his eyes. The security light was on. He started to unlock the door, but then remembered almost every horror movie he'd seen. *Don't go out there.* Instead, he walked around the house, checking to make sure all the doors and windows were locked. He grabbed the phone out of its cradle on the way back to the bedroom.

"Come on, Annie." The dog followed him, and jumped on the bed, hackles still raised. "Okay, just for tonight."

He felt safer with Annie curled up next to him. *Should look up local dog parks.* But then he imagined a whole pack of dogs, coming straight at him. *One step at a time.*

———

"Sorry I can't take you with me." Annie looked at him with baleful eyes. She nudged his hand. "I'll miss you, but I'll come home straight after the carnival. Be good." He hurried out of the house, trying not to look back.

The laughter of the children as he made them balloon elephants, giraffes, and unicorns took his mind off his lonely dog. *I love my job*, he thought. The teachers brought him savory pies, chips, root beer floats, and even cinnamon twists. The smell reminded him of Martine. She was running the face-painting booth, but every so often she would look up and smile.

Finally, the carnival crowd thinned out after the last school bell rang. Parents carried their tired children out of the gymnasium as he packed up his clown kit. Martine came over, hands smeared in paint and looking even more tired than he felt.

"How'd it go," he said, brushing a piece of paint-stained hair out of her eyes.

"It was a success. We raised so much money for the school. Thank you so much for helping out. The kids loved you, and I heard nothing but great things from the parents. They'd already asked me about having you come for summer birthday parties."

"I would like that. Listen, I'd love to see you tonight, but—"

"But, we are both very tired. I have an idea, though." She looked nervous, all of the sudden.

"Would you like to go away for the weekend with me? My sister has granted me use of her beach cottage." She rushed her words together at the end.

He felt his face paint crack as his mouth dropped open.

"If it's too sudden—"

"No, uh, I mean, that would be, I would love that." He tried to take her hand in his clown gloves.

She laughed. "It's a date, then. I'll be driving down." She kissed his cheek. "Get some sleep; it'll be an early start."

It wasn't until he got home that he remembered about poor Annie, who ran around him in circles. And that Martine needed his address. He called her, but the phone just rang and rang, without even the voice mail picking up. He hung up on the eleventh ring.

"Hope she likes dogs," he told Annie as he opened a can of dog food for her after their walk around the block. He warmed up his leftovers, humming the Italian opera from the other night. He could barely keep his eyes open as he packed his suitcase.

His head had barely touched the pillow when Annie started barking. *At least it wasn't two a.m.* Maybe he'd been too impulsive in adopting a dog. She was not only barking, but growling, jumping up on the back door, and sniffing at the crack underneath it. He looked out the door's window. The security light hadn't been triggered. Probably a rat or a raccoon.

"Annie, it's nothing. Come on to bed." She wouldn't budge, just continued barking at the door.

"Fine, then." He dragged her bed into the back room, and put her food and water bowls down. "See you in the morning. You better be good, or I'll leave you at home." She still didn't stop her growling and pawing at the back door. He hated to do it, but he had to get some sleep. *Early start, remember?* He slid the connecting door closed and locked it.

He could only faintly hear his dog barking as the room went grey and fuzzy. Enormous balloon animals chased him in his sleep.

"No," he cried out, and he woke up. His mouth felt funny, and he got up to get a drink of water. Well, he tried to, but his body wouldn't move. *Sleep paralysis, happens when you dream vivid dreams,* and he waited for it to wear off. From far away, like down a long tunnel, he could hear Annie still barking. Bang, bang, bang. She was slamming against the door. *Monday morning, first thing, back to the shelter with you.*

Wait. Something was wrong. He still couldn't move. And then he heard it. Above the distant dog barking and thuds.

Italian opera.

Humming.

Someone was there.

Martine.

She stood over him.

Kind smile.

"Shhhh, shh, shh. It's okay. It's just me."

He stopped trying to scream.

A memory. His keys.

His missing keys.

He screamed, again, but all that came out was a gurgle. And drool.

"Now, now, don't do that. You'll choke on your saliva."

She used her calm teacher voice, the one she'd used with the students earlier that day. That calm voice made it scarier when she pulled out a shiny silver knife.

"Tsk, tsk. Naughty boy. Lying to your teacher about not having a dog. Well, after I teach you a lesson, I'll go take care of it."

He felt tears blur his vision but he couldn't even blink them away. *She must have put something in his food. The restaurant leftovers?*

"It's your fault, really. Never lie to your teacher. Instead of being sent to the principal's office, though, I have a better punishment in store." She tapped the knife on the night table.

He tried. *Move.* But he couldn't even slide off the bed. She straddled him, holding the knife against his throat.

"Naughty, naughty clown."

He was going to die. At least he wouldn't feel it. *Poor Annie. I'm so sorry.* She had stopped barking. Stopped banging against the door. *Good girl.* More tears. He closed his eyes. The drug. *Whatever she'd given him must be wearing off.*

Not fast enough.

He still couldn't move.

Damn it.

Screaming. The knife falling to the floor. Dragging noises.

He couldn't see.

Silence.

Then growling.

Other noises he didn't have to see to know what they were.

He was glad he couldn't turn his head.

A thump on the bed, finally.

"Good dog," he gurgled. He felt her tail vibrate the bed.

———

Hours later, he was sitting on his front porch while crime scene investigators and police tramped through his house. An EMT had checked him over and asked if he wanted to go to the hospital.

"No," he said. He wasn't leaving Annie. They'd brought him cup after cup of hot tea. He was still shaking, though. He tried to push the sight of Martine out of his head.

Every time a cop or an investigator walked past him, they'd say "good dog" and pat Annie on the head. She never barked. Not once.

He watched the sun begin to rise over the buildings. Held onto Annie. A new day.

———

A Bad Day for a Clown

Willow Croft currently lives in the high desert, but dreams of a home by a tumultuous ocean. When she's not writing, she's caring for her rescued calico, Moon Pie.

Her work has appeared in *Rock N' Roll Horror Zine*, *Mad Scientist Journal*, *Speculative 66*, and *Neon Druid: An Anthology of Urban Celtic Fantasy*.

Find our more here: https://willowcroft.blog/ or on Twitter: https://twitter.com/WillowCroft16.

Killing Kippers

Eleanor Cawood Jones

Snow in the Midwest in January is hardly news. So it didn't make headlines on that Thursday afternoon when the temperature and dewpoint combined to dump nineteen treacherous inches of snow and ice on Green Bay, Wisconsin. Salt trucks and snowplows drove in circles, but the rest of us stayed put. Put, for me, was the Running Stick Resort and Casino. I was in town on business. The clowns, including the one on the barstool next to me, were at the end of a four-day clown convention. News to me, that clowns convened.

"Two days," Kippers the Klown moaned into her Jim Beam and ginger ale, and downed the dregs. She made a sucking noise to get every last drop and plinked the glass on the bar. "They say we'll be snowed in for at least two more days before the planes run. I'm going to miss two gigs, and I really need the money."

I made a noncommittal noise. Kippers had already told me at least six times how she would miss a Shriners' breakfast and a cat's birthday party. That's why I planned to spend the next two days hiding—hiding in the casino, in my room, in the lobby, in the parking garage, and in a bottle. (Mostly the bottle.) In short, hiding any place where Kippers wasn't.

Killing Kippers

I'd been barnacled by this wanna-be entertainer since last night, and she was shaping up to be not only seriously not funny, and in fact whiny, but an alcoholic to boot.

Kippers the (Depressing) Klown was, in fact, pickled, and had been since I'd made the mistake of asking to borrow her phone charger the night before, seated at this same bar. I'd forgotten mine and the hotel gift shop was sold out. Apparently the charger came with a price of everlasting friendship. She'd been following me around since then, showing up at breakfast and turning my time in the casino afterward into a disaster.

I calculated. If I only used my phone for essential calls, like to my therapist, who understood how I felt about being trapped in general and with clowns in particular, I could surely drag it out for another twenty-four hours before I had to borrow her charger again. Maybe in the meantime I could find a way to ditch her and her constant moaning and carrying on about how the other clowns didn't like her, the lack of work at parties, and how, if clowning was her calling, why was it all so hard?

I took a swig of my Manhattan and glanced at Kippers out of the corner (korner) of my eye. All five-foot-nothing of her. What kind of clown dresses in all-black sequins—who knew they even made sequined pantaloons?—topped by a colorful dunce cap with her short, scraggly, bleached blond hair poking out the bottom of it? The effect was black and shiny and round with a burst of color on top. Audrey Hepburn, Kippers was not. More like Tweedledee.

Or Dum. Whichever.

"My boyfriend will miss me. Who knows what he'll get into? And my poor, sick kitty needs me."

Kippers had a boyfriend? Boggled the mind. The cat I could understand. Twenty-seven cats would be even more understandable. This Klown had all the makings of a Krazy Kat Lady.

"I'm sorry about Kibbles, Kippers," I said for the seventy-second time. Kibbles the cat has gout and needs a special diet and exercise routine, according to Kippers.

Kippers turned to me as if seeing me for the first time. "You got a boyfriend back home?"

"No," I said shortly. No boyfriend, no husband. Not anymore, anyway. No cat, either. But a Manhattan? A Manhattan I did have. I took another, heftier swig and signaled Peet the bartender for a refill. (Earlier I made the mistake of asking Peet about the unusual spelling of his name on his employee badge. He told me his mom had spelled it that way so he wouldn't get confused with his twin brother, Pete. Yep, I was in Crazyland for sure.)

Soon I'd be just drunk enough to take another trip down the long hall that led to the casino. I could hear the Wheel of Riches slot machines calling my name, taunting me. This morning I'd been one pull away from a jackpot. I'd gone to find an ATM and asked Kippers, who was following me around and talking to me while I tried to play slots—not casino-savvy behavior at the best of times—to watch my machine and make sure no one touched it until I returned. She'd seen no harm in letting some guy take a turn while I was gone. He'd won the thirty grand progressive jackpot on the very next pull.

I could have used that money on a down payment for a new car and taken that trip to Hawaii I'd been promising myself for years. Maybe even paid off a credit card or two. Even after taxes.

When I came back to find the bells flashing and the guy who won cackling maniacally with glee—and cackle he well might, with all my money in his grip—Kippers was too drunk to even understand what she'd done. There was no point in explaining it to her, or beating her with the stick I could easily have snatched from the dealer at the craps table, or murdering her with my bare hands. To add insult to injury, she'd chosen that moment to lurch into me and spill her rum and coke all down the front of my one remaining clean blouse and suit jacket. At that point I simply descended into a black spiral of despair and resigned myself to starting over on another machine, staying drunk and sticky-suited, and hating all clowns everywhere forever. Especially Kippers.

And to getting out of town as soon as possible. Which brought me back to reality, which informed me in no uncertain terms that I'd be here another two days at least. I watched Peet mix my refill and then my cell phone rang.

Blessed mercy, it was my good friend Bambi. An anti-clown antidote if there ever was one.

I'd met Bambi three years before, when I'd first arrived in Green Bay to supervise the printing of an important client's direct mail fundraising campaign, consisting of billions of pieces of paper that would be inserted into millions of envelopes on a gigantic, larger-than-a-football-field printing press available only here in the Midwest. Like the casino, the press ran twenty-four hours a day.

Compared to the compact DC suburbs, everything here seemed sprawling and giant to me, including the gorgeous young woman who met me at the airport.

She had to be at least six-foot-two, with a killer body, wide blue eyes, and stick-straight, whiter-than-white hair cascading down her broad, parka-clad back. Everything about her screamed healthy outdoor activity and Scandinavian descent.

She had smiled a blinding Crest 3D White smile. "Welcome to Green Bay! I'm Bambi, and I'm with Packer Worldwide Printing." Her deep, booming voice echoed in the practically deserted airport.

Since then, I've made this same trip every three months, and Bambi and

I have grown to be close work friends and then some. She's seen me through some tough times, and I've listened to her talk about her mother-in-law, Hilda, whom we call Hitler. (And not in a nice way.) I grinned tipsily at her name on my cell phone.

I found the right button to push, held the phone up to my ear, and heard her voice rumbling out of it. "Girl, where are you right now?"

Peet plumped my drink in front of me, and I grinned at it, too. "Bar." No point in not mincing words. I was preserving my energy for the slot machines.

"Well, have Peet mix me up a gin and tonic. I'm on the way over."

"Impossible. Snow. Ice." I may have given out a little hiccup at this point. "Weather."

"No problem. I'm cross-country skiing over to see you." Of course she was. Bambi lived no more than what, five miles away? I rolled my eyes. Bad move, as Kippers came into view. I focused back on my drink.

"I was getting cabin fever," Bambi continued, gracefully ignoring the hiccup. "Figured I could use some exercise and then a drink and maybe a little round or two in the casino."

I could use some exercise, too. I pictured the long hallway between the hotel and casino, which turned in on itself twice before you arrived at that glorious, open room filled with the unique combination of buzzing and binging slot machines, shouts of eager customers, and ice-filled, clinking glasses found only in gambling establishments the world over. It was a really, really long walk to get there.

"Walking the mile, walking the mile," I mumbled into the phone.

Bambi understood. "Kippers there?" She had spent last evening with Kippers and me in the bar.

"Yeppers." I giggled.

"Well, stop drinking, and when I get there we'll get her so drunk she won't be able to follow us down to the slots. Okay?"

" 'S a plan." I found the right button and hung up on her. Things were looking up.

"Cheese curds." Peet plunked a bowl of the fried, steaming Wisconsin specialty on the bar in front of me and winked. He knew I wasn't normally much of a drinker. He probably wanted to feed me before I slid onto the floor. I sniffed the bowl. Heavenly. I reached for a curd but Kippers's mitt beat me to it. She dug out a handful and scattered most of the rest onto the bar.

I went back to my drink, waited for Bambi, and listened to Kippers smack her loathsome lips while she ate my curds.

Kippers was talking nonstop and I had half a drink left when I sensed Bambi sliding onto the barstool on the other side of Kippers. Good. We had the clown surrounded.

"Kippers, my clown friend. What's shaking?" Bambi's voice boomed, and I heard Kippers mumble something in return.

"Gin and tonic for me, Peet, and I think some hot green tea for these two clowns." I resented being included as a clown, but before I could protest, Bambi snatched something out of Kippers's gigantic purse, which was open on the bar. "Kippers, what's this?"

I peered around Kippers, who was frantically trying to retrieve something out of Bambi's man-hand.

"Diazepam?" Bambi read the label of the prescription bottle in what was, for her, a whisper. "Girl, what are you doing with this?"

Kippers gave up the fight. "The clown's life is a depressing life," she intoned dramatically. "Besides, it's just a weensy dose. You know, to take the edge off."

"Two milligrams twice a day," Bambi read aloud. She upended the bottle and shook a few into her hand. "This prescription is from last week. Why's the bottle nearly empty?"

"I've been stressed, all right? Don't know what business it is of yours anyway." Kippers took a swallow of her drink and popped another curd.

Bambi dropped the bottle back into the purse and shrugged. "Used to be a nurse."

Wow. I could imagine Bambi as a nurse. Efficient and capable, large and in charge. I bet no patient had the nerve to die on one of her shifts, either.

"Still." She moved the drinks away from Kippers and me as Peet delivered two mugs of hot tea. "Best watch the alcohol intake. You know those pills will make you sleepy on their own."

Kippers gave me a *do something* look born of alcoholic desperation, and out of the corner of my eye I could have sworn Bambi dropped one of the pills she'd palmed into the mug in front of Kippers. She moved the mug closer to the clown, and nudged her. "Tea will make you feel better. Promise."

Bambi and I made eye contact, and she read my tacit, drunken approval of her spiking Kippers's drink. The sooner this clown was out of our hair, the better.

Kippers grumbled, picked up a spoon and stirred, and took a couple of swallows of tea, then a few more until her mug was empty. I sipped mine, too. After all, I had a long walk in front of me. The heat felt good, though it was no Manhattan.

"What's dramazipipam, anyway?" Was I slurring? Surely not.

"Light tranquilizer," Bambi answered carelessly. She signaled Peet for another gin and tonic.

Kippers made some sort of noise, shoved her mug away, and put her head down on the bar with a little more force than I thought was necessary.

Peet ambled over. "Damn. That'll leave a mark."

"We'd better get her to bed," I said reluctantly. We all looked at her.

"Maybe I'd better get security to take her," Peet said. "You don't seem all that steady." He eyed Bambi. "Though I suppose Bambi could handle her solo."

I nudged Kippers. "Wake up. Bambi's going to put you to bed."

Peet leaned over. "Kippers?" He stared at Bambi. "Seriously, Bambi, is she breathing?"

And that's when all hell broke loose. Peet vaulted over the bar, knocking Kippers's purse onto the floor, and Bambi dragged me off the stool and away from Kippers. She parked me at a table, simultaneously dialing 911, and with her phone under her chin started grabbing Kippers's belongings off the floor and stuffing them into the purse, taking a moment to wipe the pill bottle on her shirt, I noticed. She requested an ambulance, tossed the purse on the table with me, and went to help Peet, who had started CPR. Others, solemn-faced, gathered around to watch and worry.

By the time emergency services arrived in the form of two EMTs hauling several cases of equipment, we were all openly speculating that it might be too late for Kippers. I wanted to weep, but the alcohol had numbed me. What if it *was* too late for her? Who would take care of her gouty cat now?

The EMTs took over, and Bambi came to sit with me. I turned to her, and she answered my unspoken question, speaking directly into my ear. "No way a dose that small would have hurt her like this. Especially that fast. It was just one pill. It may have helped her go to sleep sooner is all. But it appears to me she had a massive heart attack. Peet told me he has EMT training, and even he couldn't help her. They'll do an autopsy if she doesn't make it, you know."

I believed her. I had to. I'd seen her put the meds in Kippers's mug and hadn't done a thing to stop her. The alternative to not believing her was too painful to contemplate. Besides, she'd been a nurse. She knew about these things.

I hoped.

The EMTs were asking aloud if anyone knew whether Kippers was ill or took any medicine. Peet told them she had been drinking heavily for days, and Bambi dutifully reported that the clown had a low-dose diazepam prescription.

But it was all to no avail, and a few minutes later the EMTs stopped their efforts, covered Kippers with a thin blanket, and began to pack up their equipment. Peet, now back behind the bar, began weeping.

"Uh-oh." Bambi had given the EMTs Kippers's oversized purse once they had given up working on her. Now one of them, a tall, blond man who could have easily passed for Bambi's brother, was holding the pill bottle that had been tucked inside. He talked quietly with his partner as they stood beside Kippers's body.

"What's he saying, Bambi?"

The EMT holding the pills had opened the bottle and tipped a few pills into his hand. I thought I heard him say something along the lines of "wrong dose." What did *that* mean?

Bambi and I sat still.

His partner, a slim, dark-haired woman, answered him in a low voice. "The bottle says two milligrams."

"Well, take a gander at these pills. These are ten milligrams. Much stronger."

There was a pause. Then the female EMT whipped her phone off her belt and, dialing, left the room.

Bambi looked sick. "The pills are wrong. I bet she's gone to call the cops. Oh, my God. Ten to one Kippers poisoned herself. And all that booze on top of it."

Poisoned herself? Maybe. Unless someone switched out her pills. But I kept that thought to myself. I closed my eyes for a moment, willing myself to unsee that one extra pill slipping into the clown's drink. And unwilling to catch Bambi's eye.

Everyone in the bar was still speculating about Kippers in hushed voices when a handsome man in a suit appeared in front of our table, asking us all to go into the next room, a mini-ballroom normally reserved for special events. I supposed this qualified.

He was met with stunned silence followed by a buzz of panicked conversation. "What was it, a heart attack?" "Something must be wrong. Otherwise why would they ask us to stay?" "Foul play. It's got to be foul play." "No way! She just had too much to drink and her heart couldn't handle it."

As the handsome guy turned away from me, I could see he'd taken a tumble in the weather. The back of his coat and pants were covered in slush and mud. I resisted an urge to brush him off. It might have been misinterpreted.

Twenty or so of us followed him next door to a room filled with comfortable seating, couches, and overstuffed chairs, even a fireplace. We were all choosing seats when he beckoned for Bambi and me to follow him into a small office adjoining the main area. A uniformed police officer sat at a table with four chairs, and he asked us to join him.

The slushy (but still handsome) guy remained standing. "I'm Detective Dave DuPrey," he told us. Detective DuPrey. I filed the name away, changed it to Detective Damp Pants and shortened it to DDP in my head. (Memorization technique.) "I am told by the bartender that you two were with the deceased when she passed out."

I winced at the idea of Kippers being called "the deceased." Not that Kippers the Klown was any great shakes as a name, but it sure beat "the deceased."

He was staring directly at me.

"It's true!" Perhaps I was a little overenthusiastic. He really was incredibly good-looking. If you like that tall, dark-haired, blue-eyed type. I reminded myself he was covered in slush all over his backside.

"And who are you?"

I spread my arms in front of me. "Well, DDP. I can explain."

He raised his eyebrows.

"She's not much of drinker," Bambi offered.

"I can see that."

"Hey!" I waved my arms in case they'd forgotten I was sitting right there. "I'm just here on business. Kippers decided she'd rather hang out with me than the rest of the clowns. She had five or six drinks. Then, wham! She keeled over and her head hit the bar. We tried to wake her up to get her back to her room, and nothing. I mean, no breathing."

My voice broke and I swallowed hard. I hadn't liked Kippers. But nobody deserves to die stone drunk at a clown convention. Surrounded by, you know, clowns.

"That's when Peet hopped the bar and went to work. He told Bambi he's a trained EMT. And the EMTs got here, and then they called you."

"Okay." He flipped open his notebook. "Your name?"

"Princess."

"Your given name."

"Princess."

He waited.

"Princess Jenkins."

"Princess Jenkins?" He eyed me up and down, taking in my pin-striped suit and dress heels, highlighted hair, big brown eyes, and skinny frame. I pretended he also checked to make sure I wasn't wearing a wedding ring. His gaze lingered on the now slightly crusty rum and coke stain on my chest. "What? You a working girl?"

I sighed and gave the short version. "It was the '80s. My parents liked Prince. They wanted a boy."

He raised an eyebrow.

"I think they drank a lot."

He returned the eyebrow and turned to assess Bambi. "And you are?"

Bambi grinned at him. I was temporarily blinded by the flash of white so I didn't quite catch his expression when she offered up her name. "Bambi."

Silence.

"Bambi Swenson."

I could swear he turned pale, but he wrote Bambi's name in his notebook.

"And the deceased, what do you know about her?"

"Kippers," I confirmed.

He grimaced.

"Oh, wait." I fished in my purse for one of the dozen or so business cards Kippers had pressed on me during our brief acquaintanceship.

The card was simple, black and white, and plain, with just the words "Kippers the Klown" and a phone number on it, plus a small graphic of a circus clown in a dunce hat holding a balloon bouquet in one hand. It made the marketer in me cringe. What were her specialties? In what geographical area did she ply her trade? I knew she could do balloon animals. She gave me those, too.

"Do you think she overdosed?" I blurted out. "Or maybe someone offed her?" Hey, I watch a lot of cop TV. Maybe too much.

DDP stared. "What makes you say that?"

Oops. Maybe I shouldn't have. "We were sitting by the EMTs. We heard what they said about Kippers's pills."

"Ah. Well, anything's possible. I'm going to take everyone's statement and contact information. We'll know more in a few days. There's always an autopsy in cases like this."

"Told you so," Bambi mouthed at me.

I sighed. "Statement? I have a statement." I ignored Bambi shaking her head at me. "You know what, detective? I think Kippers was a fish out of water. Frankly, she was one of the most annoying people I've ever met and I can imagine any number of people had a boatload of reasons to kill her if it turns out that's what happened. And on top of that, she was an awful clown. I think maybe clowning wasn't her cup of tea."

Apparently I was just getting warmed up. "This was her first big convention. She said hardly any of the other clowns showed up for her ballooning class, and she didn't feel welcome at the juggling seminar, powder-base makeup session, or the keynote speech either. She didn't even fit in at the clown ministry class. She wasn't having a good time. I felt sorry for her. She felt shunned by the other clowns."

He shook his head. "Shunned by clowns. Imagine."

Bambi shook her head, too. Not to be left out, I nodded, which somehow seemed right.

"She just wanted to go home to her cat, which has gout. And her boyfriend."

"Her cat has her boyfriend?"

"No." What was with this guy? "She wanted to go home to her cat *and* her boyfriend."

"She had a boyfriend?" DDP sounded incredulous.

"I know. Hard to believe, right?" Bambi sounded sad. "Big, tall guy. She showed us a bunch of pictures on her phone. Weird-looking couple, but someone for everyone, I guess."

"Was he depressed too?" I wanted to know.

"What do you mean, was he depressed too?" The detective snapped to attention. "How well did you two actually know this clown?"

I shrugged. "Except for a couple hours I was sleeping, she's been talking nonstop to me since yesterday."

"I just met her last night," Bambi said. "But tonight I saw she had that prescription you already know about for diazepam in her purse. It was for a tiny dose, according to the label on the bottle, but still, not what you'd find in a purse every day."

"A clown's life is a hard life," I intoned dramatically. Perhaps wisely, they both ignored me.

"And you'd know this because?" The detective looked at Bambi.

She shrugged. "I used to be a nurse a long time ago. So I know a bit about meds. But the shift work and patients got to me after a while. I do PR for Packer Worldwide Printing now."

Detective DuPrey eyed her again. "I bet you were a good nurse. Okay, I'll call the number on the card and see if I can't get hold of the boyfriend." He sighed. "So I'm finishing with Princess and Bambi and next up I have"—he consulted his notebook—"Bobbles and Wobbles, with their twin clown act." He glanced around. "When are Dopey, Grumpy, Doc, and Sweepy going to show up?"

"Sleepy," I said.

He gave me a strange look. "Well, yeah, it's late. I'm sure you are."

"No. Sleepy. The dwarf. Not Sweepy."

"Hunh. You sure?"

"Sure as shootin'," I told him. At this point I absolutely did *not* hiccup.

"Hunh," he said again. He opened the door and stuck his head out. "Okay, I'm through interviewing these two. Now send in the clowns." He turned and cut his eyes to me, waiting.

Was that a cue for me to sing? I sat up and took a breath, but Bambi poked me in the back. Hard.

"Funny," I heard Bambi rumble behind me. Good old Bambi.

He gave me a little nod and I swear that eyebrow quirked again, then we were out the door. There were a dozen or so clowns draped about the party room waiting to be interviewed. I grabbed Bambi's hand and bolted before one of them could offer to make me a balloon giraffe or juggle scarves at me.

We wound up—where else?—back at the bar.

We were a glum bunch. I worried the detective would find out that Kippers had cost me a jackpot in the casino that very morning. Bambi worried someone else besides me may have seen her put that tiny pill in the clown's tea. Even Peet was worried. It turns out Kippers hadn't tipped him as much as one red cent, and he'd told several people at the bar that people like her were so miserable they were better off dead. Ouch. But I figured the way Peet had leaped over the bar to perform CPR on Kippers sort of took him out of the running as a suspect.

And was it my imagination or did the clowns who came back to the bar after giving their statements to DDP all seem highly nervous? (Well, I mean, more nervous than clowns usually seem.) Rumors were already spreading about the pill bottle in Kippers's purse. Was it Kippers herself who had switched her pills? Or did someone do it without her knowledge? Did one of these clowns dislike her to that extent? And why?

Killing Kippers

Like DDP had said in all his damp-panted wisdom, anything was possible.

Anything at all. Especially with this bunch of clowns who, along with us, closed down the bar before we all eventually straggled off to get some sleep, Bambi taking the spare bed in my double room.

And speaking (again) of clowns, I had to revise my opinion of clowns in general before I left Green Bay. The conference clowns, spearheaded by the ones who had been in the bar with us, held a short memorial for Kippers the next night in the long hall between the hotel and the casino. It was a touching service, with a moving speech by the convention president and a demonstration of balloon animal crafting by the few clowns who had been in Kippers's class.

The clowns I met are quite serious about their profession. Most have gone through years of training, not only for professional gigs but for volunteer work at children's hospitals and charity events. Many are third- and fourth-generation clowns. Some had even been planning to mentor Kippers on her techniques. They were well aware she was feeling left out. Great people. And, as I said, a very touching, very professional memorial service.

All the clowns and several hotel employees came, plus Bambi and me, and I'd like to think it wasn't because we were all still snowed in and had nothing better to do. DDP came too, in a clean suit this time.

And two days later, without learning anything new, we all finally flew home. Well, all of us except Kippers.

Bambi called a week later with the news that we were all red herrings in the demise of Kippers. We were, in fact, saved by the autopsy.

"So, guess what, Princess? Turns out Kippers was loaded up with so much diazepam that it's amazing she didn't keel over before we had that last drinking session in the bar."

"Oh, wow. You sure?" I was relieved and sad at the same time.

"I'm e-mailing you the link to the story in the paper this morning," Bambi said. She paused and I could hear her fingernails clicking on her keyboard. "According to this, there's no way she should have had that much tranquilizer in her system, even if she'd swallowed the entire bottle of pills she had with her. She must have been high as a kite before she even arrived at the convention."

I opened my e-mail and scanned the story while she was talking. The reporter had interviewed Detective DuPrey, who had retrieved the meds from Kippers's purse and confirmed that indeed the pills labeled two milligrams on the bottle were actually ten milligrams.

"According to the prescription bottle you saw, Kippers should have been taking only four milligrams a day," I said. "But she must have been taking at least twenty and probably a lot more. I wonder if we'll ever know exactly how many pills she was taking to cope with her stress at the convention. And you saw how she liked to drink." I shuddered. In spite of my best intentions, I still didn't like to remember being surrounded by clowns.

"No kidding," Bambi said. "Well, I think you're the one who accidentally sent Detective DuPrey in the right direction when you asked if Kippers's boyfriend had been depressed too."

"Maybe so," I agreed. Turns out the boyfriend, Wallace (not a clown, but in fact a casino employee in Las Vegas where he and Kippers lived) had been taking large doses of diazepam and he had switched his own pills with Kippers's. The two-milligram-sized pills were found in Wallace's medicine cabinet, in his own prescription bottle.

I read on. The reporter quoted Wallace during his confession as saying, "I didn't mean to kill her. I just wanted her to relax so she would shut up. Is that a crime?" There was a picture of a distraught-looking man waving his hands about. He was a big, tall guy, like I remembered from Kippers's photos. I could see why he'd need a giant dose of tranqs. Especially living with Kippers and Gouty.

"I never would have confessed if I was Wallace," Bambi said, bringing me back to the present moment. "I'd have said Kippers switched the pills herself."

I agreed with Bambi. I would have accused Kippers of making the pill switch and then I would have lawyered up. (As I mentioned, I watch a lot of crime television since the divorce and I'm a bit of an expert at police lingo. And I know my rights.) Still, it was a crime and the charge would be involuntary manslaughter.

To tell you the truth, my sympathies were with Wallace.

Meanwhile, I knew one marketing director, one publicity employee, one bartender, and a whole bunch of (nervous) clowns who were all no doubt secretly breathing sighs of relief that they wouldn't be labeled as murder suspects in the death of Kippers the Klown. Because, let's face it, there's nothing funny about that. And as for one extra pill in a mug of tea playing a role in the clown's demise, I am almost one hundred percent certain it made not a whit of difference.

"Has Detective DuPrey called you?" I could hear the smile in Bambi's voice. "I mean, in an unofficial capacity, now that none of us are on his suspect list anymore."

She couldn't see me blushing. "What would make you think that?"

Shortly after charges were filed against Wallace, DDP attended a forensics conference in my neck of the woods in the Virginia suburbs of our nation's capital. He came down for four days at the end of February and ended up staying an extra four days. Seems there were some sights he wanted to see. And I know DC very, very well.

I've been up to Green Bay twice since then, once for business and once to stay with Bambi and her husband, Lars, so she could teach me how to cross-country ski on what she calls my matchstick legs. Next time, she says, we're going to the firing range so I can learn to handle a gun properly before she takes me hunting. (And don't think the twenty-five-ways-to-Sunday irony of going hunting with someone named Bambi escapes me, either.) Bambi has formed an impression I might move to Wisconsin permanently, and she's appointed herself my self-sufficiency and survival coach.

During both recent visits I spent a lot more time with DDP. He has two kids he's raising by himself. Seems his ex didn't like being married, much less to a detective. Shelley is four and Matthew is eight.

Shelley demanded to know why I was named Princess, and I may or may not have allowed her to believe that if I was not, in fact, a Disney princess, I was at least related to them. (The word "cousin" may have been used.)

And I may or may not have memorized the performance statistics of the entire Green Bay Packers starting lineup to impress a certain precocious eight-year-old with eyes just like his daddy's. (That part was easy. I'm in marketing and we eat statistics for breakfast.)

I never imagined myself as a potential stepmother. Then again, I never imagined myself missing a casino jackpot by a buck, aiding and abetting in accidentally offing a clown, or bagging a deer with a woman named Bambi. So I'm keeping an open mind.

Stranger things have happened.

Killing Kippers

Heck, maybe someday I'll even tell him why I call him DDP. Then again, maybe Detective Damp Pants never needs to know.

Eleanor Cawood Jones began writing in elementary school, using #2 pencils to craft crime stories starring her stuffed animals. Her short stories have appeared in a variety of venues, including *Malice Domestic 13: Mystery Most Geographical*, *Florida Happens*, and *Crimes: Invitation to Murder*.

A former newspaper reporter and reformed marketing director, Eleanor is a Tennessee native who lives in Northern Virginia and travels often. You'll find her rearranging furniture or lurking at airports.

Naughty

Ben Fitts

"Hello boys and girls, are you ready to laugh?" exclaimed Poodles, his real mouth grinning inside the smile painted on his face. Poodles didn't have to fake the smile. He genuinely loved being a clown.

Unfortunately, people tended not to love having him be a clown.

"You're spooky," whined a girl in pigtails sitting in the dirt. "Why do you have eyes painted around your eyes and a mouth painted around your mouth? Can't you just have your real eyes and real mouth?"

Poodles stopped dead in his routine and looked at the dozen or so children assembled before him in the backyard. Clowning might invite more heckling than any other form of performance, but somehow Poodles never managed to really get used to it.

"Because it's *ggggooooooofffffyyyyy!*" he declared at last after too long a pause, accentuating the word with a squeak of a handheld horn. The response was met with a stoic silence from the children. They stared at him with dead, unamused eyes.

"No, it makes you look like your face is being eaten by another face," piped a bespectacled boy who didn't even look up from the ants he was squishing beneath his sneakers. At this, the children did laugh.

It was the sort of hearty, unforced laughter that unappreciated clowns like Poodles only dream of summoning.

"Now why would you say that?" he asked in his exaggerated clown voice. "That hurts my *ffffffeeeeeelllllliiiinnnggggssss.*"

He ran one gloved finger down his cheek to indicate a falling tear and blew on a slide whistle. It was no better received than his last retort.

"Alright, boys and girls, do you want to hear some jokes?" he asked earnestly, hoping to move along into his prepared act.

"No," said the girl in pigtails, "I don't know why my parents even got you. I don't even like clowns."

"So you're the birthday girl?" asked Poodles, turning his buoyant attention to the little girl. "What would you like to see me do then?"

"Nothing," she pouted. "I wanted a *piñata*, but my stupid parents got me you instead."

"Now, now," he said, wagging an index finger. "You really shouldn't call your parents stupid. That's not very nice, now is it?"

"Oh fuck off, you dumb clown."

Poodles painted jaw dropped.

His act was rarely well received even by clown standards, and his perpetually and unforced cheery attitude could infuriate, but he had never before been cursed out by a nine-year-old at her own birthday party.

Poodles was similarly rosy when he wasn't wearing his costume or makeup and the world called him Jeff McKenzie. He was the kind of man who clicked the remote to a new channel when the news on CNN was too gloomy, whose home was decorated with Norman Rockwell prints, and who read primarily children's books even though he was well into adulthood and had no children of his own.

He had tried reading adult literature, but had found it far too glum. He hadn't even made it thirty pages into *The Scarlet Letter* before having to put the novel down, on the verge of tears. He hadn't minded Hester's public shaming too much, although it was certainly unpleasant, but the thought of the little baby Pearl growing up without knowing whom her father was was just too much for him.

He preferred sunnily illustrated books about saintly children and anthropomorphized animals that reminded him of the safety he had felt as a child before the realities of the real world fully dawned on him. The life of Jeff McKenzie could be a scary place but when he was Poodles, the world was like something out of the mind of P.D. Eastman. Until it wasn't.

"I'll ask you not to use such language, young lady," he said as sternly as he could muster. "A place with a clown is a happy place, and therefore not a place for ugly words like that."

"Blow it out your ass, faggot," retorted a boy who was multitasking between picking snot out of his nose and chewing on a helpless ladybug. That word made Poodles' blood boil.

He had been called that slur more time than he dared to count, both as Poodles and as Jeff. The fact that he wasn't actually gay didn't seem to deter the insult. Well, he was petty sure he wasn't gay. He had never had sex with another man, so he thought that must count for something, but he had never had sex with a woman either so it probably counted for less than it could have.

The idea of being intimate in that way with someone felt icky to Jeff. The only people whom we knew of even having seen his penis had been his parents and some of his doctors, and the thought of moist genitals interlocking with each other always left him a little queasy. The word "naughty" always came to mind.

Naughty

As a child, he had been terrified of his parents calling him naughty. Naughty had meant bad, so a young Jeff had reasoned that if he avoided being naughty he would therefore be good. He didn't say bad words or steal dessert from the cupboard or watch PG-13 movies when they were on cable or do anything of the other things his mother and father had labeled as "naughty". He kept himself afloat in a filthy world by knowing that he was pure and virtuous and better than the ugly things he saw around him. It was his philosophy as a child and remained his philosophy through his teenage years and into adulthood.

"That word is more than ugly. It's *hateful*," he lectured the boy. "Why would you use it? What have gay people ever done to hurt you?"

"What's a gay people?" the boy asked as he swallowed what remained of the ladybug's thorax.

"It's a... well... sometimes when two people..." he began to stammer, but then realized the boy was no longer paying attention. He was busy shoving a wad of snot from his nose up the nostril of a nearby and much smaller child. The smaller child struggled half-heartedly. It looked mostly for show.

Poodles sighed. If he had not been a tenacious man, he would have given up clowning years ago. He liked to begin his routine with some jokes, but the time for those had clearly passed. It was time to bring out the big guns and hit the children with the most exciting thing is his entire clownish repertoire.

"Who wants to see some balloon animals?"

"Lame," said a girl with home-cut bangs who was tossing pebbles at some squirrels in a nearby tree. The squirrels squealed and scurried away as the tiny rocks struck them.

Ignoring this, Poodles trotted to his gym bag laying on the grass and gathered up a bag of balloons. He withdrew a skinny green balloon and inflated it with several exaggerated huffs. It swelled into life and Poodles began to work on it with a series of squeaky twists.

Several of the children covered their ears and griped about the noise. Poodles understood that to a certain degree. The shrill noise of the rubber-latex blend scraping against itself gotten on his nerves as well when he first started clowning, but he had pushed the discomfort aside because it was a tiny sacrifice to make for something as wonderful as a balloon animal. He wished the children would understand that.

"And voila!" he declared, holding a green balloon dog to the children. "Who wants a brand new puppy?"

"You suck at this," said a girl in a T-shirt with Spongebob Squarepants grinning face emblazoned across it. "I can make balloon animals way better than you. Watch!"

The girl dashed the bag of balloons resting beside Poodles oversized clown shoe. He held her off with one gloved hand. She was surprisingly strong for her size, but that size wasn't much larger than several chinchillas stacked on top of each other.

"Where have all the adults gone?" he demanded as he fended off the child.

"My parents are in their room upstairs," said the birthday girl. "They're banging."

"What? How do you know that?" he asked, the words tumbling out of his mouth before he had time to consider them.

"Because when you got all of out here I heard my mommy tell my daddy, 'The clown is starting, we can go upstairs bang now', so that's how I know."

"Oh, well that's quite enough about that. Sorry I ask..."

"And then my daddy said 'Yes please!' and started looking all happy," the girl continued. "Then my mommy slid her underwear off from under her skirt and threw it at my daddy's face, where it landed and hung off his nose for a little bit. He just let it lay there for a moment, but then he held it in his teeth and picked my mommy up and carried her upstairs and then I heard..."

"Alright, enough!" Poodles shouted. If it wasn't for the white paint slathered on his face, his cheeks would have burning bright red. Hearing adults talk about sex made him feel uncomfortable and dirty. Hearing nine-year-olds talk about it was like having a blood vessel pop in his brain.

"Don't yell at me," the girl pouted. "It's my birthday and you're *my* clown. That means you have to do what I say."

"It does not," informed Poodles.

"Yes it does, bitch!" shrieked the girl. "I wanted a *piñata* for my birthday but all I got was you, so you're going to be my *piñata*. What've we got to hit him with?"

"I saw a shovel in that shed over there," said the boy who had been eating a ladybug.

"Go get it for me," the girl instructed. "It's my birthday, so I get the first swing."

The boy scurried off to the shed to obey the command.

"Alright, children," said Poodles, one hand still deflecting the girl in Spongebob T-shirt as she tried to get at his bag of balloons. "You've shown yourself to be a rotten, naughty bunch if I may say so, but you are not about to beat me with a shovel. You may be misbehaved, but you are still just children. You're not old enough yet to be *evil*."

The boy returned from the shed with a big, two-handed flat shovel.

"Don't we need to blindfold you or something?" he asked as he handed her the shovel.

"No. It's my birthday so I make the rules, and I want to see this little bitch *squirm*."

Gripping the shovel like a baseball bat, she swung at Poodles. The shovel's rusty blade connected solidly with his kneecap.

Poodles collapsed onto the ground, screaming and holding his bloody leg. Tears poured out his eyes and smudged his face paint. He tried to speak; all that came out was an incomprehensible gurgle.

"I want a turn with the shovel!" whined the boy who had been stepping on ants.

"Not until I break him open. That's how the rules of *piñata* work," explained the birthday girl, whipping another blow with the shovel across Poodles' prone body. This one landed on his chest and tore open his baggy striped shirt, revealing his sunken chest.

A second strike to the spot tore the skin open and spilled blood over his costume.

Regaining some of his composure, Poodles tried to stand but the rest of the children held him down. Jeff McKenzie had never been an athletic man, and the combined strength of all the children was more than he could resist in his wounded state.

"Don't let the *piñata* getaway!" shrieked the boy who had been eating a ladybug. A pair of grubby hands ripped away what remained of Poodles' shirt, leaving an exposed target of pale flesh.

The birthday girl lifted the shovel high over her head, aimed her attack, and swung down. The blade of shovel buried deep into his stomach. The brought the shovel down again and again, eventually tearing open the flesh, exposing parts of him that had no business ever seeing the light of day.

Poodles felt fingers reaching into the crater of his stomach. With what little energy he had left, he craned his neck up to see the girl in the Spongebob T-shirt holding a severed segment of his intestine.

"I told you I'm way better at balloon animals than you!" she proclaimed. "See? It's a snake."

Naughty

"You children are all very, *very* naughty," Poodles said with his dying breath.

Ben Fitts is a writer, musician, and zinester from New York. He is the creator of the zines *The Rock N' Roll Horror Zine*, *A Beginner's Guide To Bizarro Fiction* and *Choose Your Own Death*, and his short fiction has appeared in a number of publications.

Life of the Party

Casey Douglass

"I didn't kill those kids!"

"Such an original line, I've not heard that one before!"

"I didn't!"

"And yet you're the one chained to this table, pissing off the very person who might just believe you if you'd only sit still and cooperate!"

There was the slight clink of a chain settling against a metal table top.

"That's better, Mr. Blythe."

"Bask."

"Excuse me?"

"Bask. It's my clowning name, and it feels more like me than my other one."

"Okay. Bask. It makes no difference to me, as long as your legal name is in the record. I'm Detective Font. We are being observed through that mirror over there, and you are being recorded on the machine just below it. Am I right that you've refused legal representation?"

"Yes."

"That's your choice. Being only myself here, there is no good cop bad cop routine, just tell me straight what happened, in your own time, and I'll pipe in with questions when I need clarification on something, sound fair?"

"Yes."

"Good. To get us started, tell me how you came to be at the party on Green Street yesterday afternoon, how were you hired?"

"A woman approached me in a pub. The Boatsman, I think it was."

"You aren't sure of the name? Were you drunk?"

"Not particularly. That's not to say that I don't drink. I have a bit of a problem with it. I can't remember the name of the place because I've only been in town a few days."

"Oh? Where were you before?"

"The capital."

"And why did you leave?"

"I was performing at a party a few months ago. A kid got hurt doing something stupid, and the parents, rather than blame themselves, decided to blame me. They spread all sorts of lies about me and ruined my reputation. I came here to make a fresh start."

"Somewhere where nobody knows you…"

"Exactly."

"Why did you come here in particular?"

"I didn't choose it for any particular reason, I just pointed to a random place on the map and this was it. Well… if I'm really honest, I woke up one morning and the neck of an empty beer bottle was pointing here. I'm an idiot for being superstitious. Especially after what's happened now."

"We'll get to that. You said you have a drink problem?"

"One I've been working on for five years now."

"Did anything bring it about?"

"Divorce. Not being allowed to see my kids."

"You didn't drink before then?"

"No more than most people, high days and holidays mainly."

"Can I ask why you split with your wife?"

"She fell out of love with me, but that soon turned to hatred for reasons I still don't understand."

"I'm sorry."

"Yeah, me too."

"You clowned then?"

"Oh, I have since I was a teen. I love it. Even now, it's the last thing left that I'm any good at. I don't drink on the job though, if that is where your mind is going."

"We know you don't or you wouldn't be sitting and breathing opposite me would you?"

"No, I guess not. I guess my point is, sure, I'm a drunken idiot, but clowning is as real as things get for me, it's my calling. However much I drink or fuck up when I'm not working, when it's time to get the laughs and put on a show, I pop into my groove and knock it out of the park. I'm a damn good clown, just a shitty human being."

"I'm sure. Now, rolling things back to the pub-'

"Clowning is the only break I have in my drinking. I mean, I'd be dead without that wouldn't I? Besides the other thing?"

"Yes you might be Mr er... Bask. But if we could return to the pub?"

"Yes?"

"The woman?"

"Oh yes! Miss Smith!"

"You said that she approached you?"

"Yes she did! She wanted to hire me to do a show."

"How did she know you were a clown?"

"I had just finished a show not half an hour earlier. I couldn't be bothered to change so I was still half in consume, saving my nose and hat, which I'd left in the car."

"I see. What did she look like?"

"Hmm. Well, she was slim, dark hair, piercing eyes. I guess she was about thirty? Maybe anything up to forty. I'm terrible at guessing ages I'm afraid."

"That's good enough, it's a tough thing sometimes."

"I don't know why I'm struggling. She was quite memorable in many ways."

"Such as?"

"Well, wanting me to do a free show. Stalking me later for another!"

"Try not to jump too far ahead. Let's start with the free show... what did she say?"

"She said that she knew me, that she'd heard about me from a friend in the capital."

"How did she know it was you?"

"I guess my costume. We clowns like to dress differently to each other, to be distinctive in some way. That and me downing drink after drink while dressed as a clown. I don't rightly know how she knew it was me for certain, that I'd only just come into town, and what I'd left behind, but she did. She mentioned the kid who lost an arm, so I knew that she knew who I was."

"The kid that got hurt lost an arm?"

"Yes. A bouncy castle too near a climbing frame in the garden is a bad idea. He jumped too high, fell out of the castle and got his arm stuck between two angles of the frame. He lost it because they had to amputate it later in hospital. Turned green or something."

"Holy shit!"

"That's my sentiment too. As I said, the parents blamed me. Apparently the fact that they were fucking each other upstairs in the bedroom for almost an hour seemed to be lost on them. I mean Jesus, the bouncy castle was behind where they'd made the stage! How could I keep a watch on that and do the show? There was no other adult supervision either! Morons!"

"So... Miss Smith had her man..."

"Yeah. She basically told me that she was putting on a party and that she'd like me to perform for free. I laughed in her face and told to her run along."

"And then she blackmailed you?"

"She threatened to yes. Said she'd make it known who I was and where I'd come from, that no one would hire me again."

"Wouldn't they have found out anyway, eventually? Seeing as you dress distinctively and all that?"

"I was about to change my costume to something new, but that first gig had landed in my lap when I needed the money, and I'd had no time to come up with a new look."

"A little sloppy though wasn't it?"

"Drink was more important..."

"It was unlucky to be recognised so quickly I'll admit. What happened next, with Miss Smith?"

"Well, she huffed and stormed out."

"That's it?"

"At that point, yes. After I finished my drink I went to my flat to get some sleep. I'd not locked the door for more than thirty seconds when there was a knock."

"Let me guess..."

"Yes. The crazy bitch flashed me with an old Polaroid camera, just at the moment I opened the door."

"What then?"

"She barged in, throwing some papers on the coffee table, telling me she wasn't bluffing. She had me over a barrel."

"Papers?"

"Newspapers, the ones that covered the kid amputation thing. Some had used my picture. She held up the Polaroid photo and said it would be put onto flyers next to the old article before the night was out, and the flyers would be on every lamppost from here to, well, everywhere."

"If you don't mind me saying Bask, someone your size, being provoked like that... I wouldn't have been surprised if you'd grabbed the photo and pushed her out of your room. You'd have had the right, she was the one breaking the law. I'm not saying you should have hit her you understand, but you could have acted."

"I know. Maybe if I'd been less tired, had drunk a bit less, I'd have been able to keep my mind on the present moment. Instead, I was taken in by her threats, seeing myself never clowning again. I've got a damn good imagination, I'm good at scaring myself, let alone when I'm being threatened. I guess it took the Polaroid and articles shoved in my face to actually believe her. So I said I'd do it."

"What did she do after that?"

"She gathered the papers up again and trotted out of the room, but not before she'd left a note with the time and address of the party the next day."

"And you did the party..."

"And I did the party. Can we take a break? I need to pee."

"I hope your toilet break suitably refreshed you?"

"Yes thanks. Nice to stretch my legs to be honest."

"Then I should have your full attention for the next bit."

"You do."

"Okay, the party... What time did you get there?"

"It was just after one in the afternoon. I know because I'd just heard the news on the radio as I drove over."

"Did you notice anything amiss when you pulled up at the house?"

"Not a thing. There were a few balloons tied to the porch, and I could hear kids playing somewhere behind the house. So all normal on that front."

"Did you knock on the front door or go straight around the back?"

"I went straight around. Didn't think I'd be heard with all the ruckus."

"What did you see when you entered the back garden?"

"I saw a swimming pool, that's the first thing I saw. Beyond it was a tent-thing with the sides open."

"A marquee?"

"Maybe, that sounds right. I guess I should really know that shouldn't I. I forget sometimes. There was a table inside it with presents and food and that kind of thing."

"So it was a birthday party?"

"I guess so. Miss Smith didn't exactly tell me much the night before."

"Where was she when you arrived?"

"She was supervising the kids."

"Were there any other adults around?"

"At the start there seemed to be, but as the afternoon went on, I saw them leave."

"Didn't that strike you as a bit strange? Parents leaving their kids alone?"

"I was wrapped up in doing my show by then. I realised just about the same time as I noticed there seemed to be less kids around."

"Do you know what time that was?"

"Tough to say. I mean, my show is about an hour long... I was a good half way through when things started to seem a bit quiet. The kids that were there were pretty dopey too, some were asleep on the floor."

"But you carried on?"

"It was a hot day you understand, and Miss Smith was staring daggers at me any time I paused for breath."

"What did she do the other times, the times when you weren't taking a breather?"

"I was too busy to see."

"Hmm."

"Hey, clowning is an engrossing job, and you always focus on one kid at a time, trying to get them to laugh or take part, whatever. It can make you a bit blinkered, and I guess the stress of being blackmailed into the fucking thing didn't help much either!"

"I can't imagine."

"No you fucking can't!"

"Relax. Take a breath. I'm here to help you, to get your side of things, but if you irritate me I'll get annoyed, and then I might struggle to see your side so clearly..."

The tick-tocks of the wall clock echoed around the room.

"Shall we continue?"

"Okay."

"So you finished your act?"

"Yes, I did the whole thing."

"And how many children were still watching you at this point?"

"Err, I'd say a handful."

"Could you give me a number?"

"Ten maybe?"

"Out of...?"

"Twenty, maybe twenty five when I started."

"Jesus."

"Like I said, I was focussed on the act more than anything."

"Uh-huh. So when did Miss Smith appear again?"

"I'd say about the time I turned the music off."

"She brought you the drink then?"

"Yes. A big frosty glass of beer."

"Why didn't you drink it?"

"I was still on the clock, so to speak. I might drink the second I get in a bar or through my own door, but I was still on the premises of a job, even a non-paying job."

"So you refused it?"

"Yes."

"How did she react?"

"She looked really pissed off. I know why now."

"Yes. We haven't got the results back from the lab yet but we suspect a pretty nasty cocktail of stuff in that beer."

"I guess I'd be too dead to interview if I'd downed it."

"More than likely."

"Did she give the same thing to the kids?"

"We don't think so. We think they were still alive when they were moved."

"Moved? I thought she killed them there!"

"No. Well, she did one or two. The working theory is she was going to make you the fall guy, buy herself some time."

Bask looked down at the table. "So you know it wasn't me!"

"We do, but we had to interview you to see if you were in on it and were just double-crossed."

"Even though I didn't do it, I still fucked up didn't I?"

"I'd say so."

Bask blew the air out through his pursed lips. "The bitch got me both ways. I can't clown again, not with this hanging over me. Shit, I mean I know it's about the kids and I probably sound like a selfish prick, but..."

"But?"

"I'm done. My life is over now, there's nothing left for me to hope for."

"I'm sure there will be something-'

"Could you bring me that drink now? The one being tested? I have a feeling that it's the only drink in the world that would actually satisfy the urge I'm feeling right now."

"I'm sorry."

"Fuck you!"

Casey Douglass is a fully fledged geek who enjoys writing about technology, entertainment, and geek culture, as well as the deeper topics of life.

He writes in a number of genres including horror, sci-fi and fantasy, but his creations share a thread of unease that winds through the characters or the situations in which they find themselves.

Find out more here: https://www.casey-douglass.com/

The Killer Clown Massacre

Simon Petersen

*People call it the great clown panic or clown uprising of 2016.
And so far it shows no sign of abating.*

—The Guardian, 31 October 2016

1

In an ironic twist, akin to Chinese alchemists inventing gunpowder while attempting to find an elixir to immortality, it began as a lesson about the history of clowns at Somers Point Community College in Atlantic County, New Jersey. There, inside one of the school's austere grey buildings, first-year professor Paul Cox had his students enthralled with another of his patented lectures on the origins of popular culture.

"From Pennywise the Dancing Clown to the creepy clown under the bed in *Poltergeist* and everything in between and since, the so-called 'evil clown' is a subversion of the traditional circus clowns of the 19th and 20th centuries." Hands shot up around the large auditorium as Professor Cox, wearing black-rimmed glasses and an ugly brown blazer in an apparent effort to look more like his much older peers, paused to take a swig from a plastic drink bottle. He brushed his long blond hair out of his face with his free hand, before placing the bottle back on the wooden lectern in front of him.

"I know what you're thinking," he said, finally continuing with his lecture. "Yes, yes, *yes*, clowns are indeed *much* older than this, of course, but for our pop cultural purposes we don't need to look back to the ancient clowns of the Fifth dynasty of Egypt, which served socio-religious and psychological roles, or even the court jesters from the medieval and Renaissance eras."

The hands fell back down again. Many of them picked up pens and started frantically writing notes, while others tapped away on laptops.

"And what caused this subversion of the beloved circus clown? Hmmm? Anyone?" Professor Cox looked around the room. All eyes were on him, and yet no-one ventured an answer to his question. "Do you think Stephen King is to blame for coulrophobia? That means a fear of clowns, in case you were wondering." He smiled, brushing the hair out of his face once more. "I must admit, Pennywise scared the bejesus out of me when I was a kid. Or was Batman's nemesis, The Joker, the first 'scary clown' in pop culture? The Joker made his debut way back in 1940, before even I was born."

The joke earned only the half-hearted laughter that it deserved. It would have worked better if Professor Cox wasn't already the college's youngest professor by nearly a decade, and only a few years older than most of his students. His relatively young age and the subject matter of his lectures ensured his classes were always overprescribed.

In the front row of the lecture theatre, a single hand shot skyward. Its owner, a young athletic-looking man in a fitted white polo shirt, a slick black pompadour resting proudly above his princely features, looked as though he would haemorrhage in his seat if the professor didn't immediately call on him.

"Yes, Billy," said Professor Cox, pointing at the student down the front of the auditorium.

"What about American serial killer John Wayne Gacy, sir? He used to dress up as a clown at children's birthday parties." Like someone who'd just passed a kidney stone, Billy sounded relieved to blurt out that scrap of information to the auditorium.

"You might be right, but..."

"He called himself Pogo," continued Billy, blithely unaware that he had interrupted his professor. "He'd attend events for charity, and he even visited sick children in the hospital in his clown getup, all the while he was raping and torturing his victims. He'd eventually murder them by asphyxiation or strangulation and stuff them in the crawl space of his home."

For the first time since the lecture began, most of the class' eyes were no longer on the professor, but on Billy, who seemed to relish the opportunity to talk-up Gacy as someone would their favourite musician or professional sportsperson. For his part, the young arts and humanities major continued to stare at his professor, locking eyes, a bombastic smile on his face as he continued to wax lyrical about the infamous serial killer.

"He killed 33 people," Billy continued. "That we know of, sir. It could have been more. A lot more. Gacy himself once said that he'd been the 'judge, jury and executioner of many, many people'. He also once said that 'clowns can get away with murder'. Well, I guess he was wrong about that one."

Sporadic laughter rippled through the auditorium, as much in disbelief as actual amusement. Professor Cox wasn't smiling, though. The young professor was frowning into his lecture notes. "That's quite enough," he said. "Now, where were we again…"

"He was eventually convicted, of course, before spending 14 years on death row, waiting for the lethal injection that would end him. Now, do you know what Gacy's final words were before his execution on 10 May 1994?"

"Okay, I said that's enough, Billy. We don't have time for this. Moving right along…"

"Kiss my ass." Billy grinned. "I mean that's what his last words were. Sorry, professor. I didn't mean you."

The tension finally broke under the weight of Billy's impudence, and the auditorium filled with laughter. Even the lecturer couldn't suppress a small smile. "I like your work, Billy. Really, I do. But can I please finish my lecture now?" He checked his watch. "We're running short on time."

Pausing for a moment to think back to where he left off, Professor Cox decided to skip the rest of the history lesson and launch right into the topic du jour. "Rather than being just another garden-variety craze, such as the planking fad of 2010-11 or the ice bucket challenge in 2015, the current clown panic is more than just skin deep. It's rooted in our collective psyche thanks to Pennywise, The Joker, and yes, even John Wayne Gacy."

Some students laughed again as Billy gave his lecturer a little wave.

"Now, why would a bunch of people want to dress up as clowns to scare people? There is no definitive answer for that, but I think the 'virality' of this behaviour, the reason why it's spread far and wide, is largely due to the fact that clowns are, essentially, just really rather frightening."

As the electric bell rang in the hallway outside, marking the sudden death of the morning and the birth of the afternoon, Professor Cox had to shout to give his final thoughts on the matter of killer clowns and susceptible teens while everyone else in the auditorium packed away their belongings.

"The potent mix of intense feeling about scary clowns, mixed with the irrepressible power of social media and popular culture, has created this unique cultural phenomenon. And I doubt we've seen the end of this one just yet, folks. Now, take care, I'll see you all next time. Don't forget to hand-in your essays on the way out, if you haven't already."

That was all his students needed to start hurrying to the exits, beyond which lay lunch and afternoon classes. On the way out, Billy doffed an invisible cap to his professor, who was too busy collecting essays from some of his students to notice.

Jamie Walsh was waiting for Billy outside of the second-story lecture theatre, leaning against the wall with his backpack on the floor beside him. A tall good-looking lad from a well-to-do upper-class family, it may as well have been the world at his feet, not his college gear. With grades to match his appearance, it was supposed to be only a matter of time before the commerce major joined his old man at the family business, a big-time pharmaceuticals firm with offices across Europe and North America.

Jamie slow-clapped when he saw his friend approaching. "What a performance. You had me and everyone in stitches at the end, but *damn* it looked like shit was getting dark for a moment there. Professor Cox is going to think you're a total nut-job psycho, and he'd be right on the money, my bro. You're a certified lunatic."

"Glad you enjoyed it," said Billy, proudly showing off every one of his perfectly white teeth in a wide smile. "Just setting the tone for this evening, my friend."

Jamie's face flickered like a short burst of interference on a satellite broadcast. "We're not really still going through with this, are we?"

"You bet your ass we are. Why do you ask? You going to wimp out on me, you pussy?"

"No way, bro. Me, Derek, Smithy, and Steve are all keen. Drinks at our place first, right?" It was a rhetorical question. They wouldn't have the balls to don killer-clown masks and frighten hundreds of people at an open-air showing of Halloween in the park without being fucked up on something.

"Good. This is going to be a night to remember."

Indeed, it would be, for all those who survived it.

2

Hank Wilcox and his cronies were spoiling for a fight before they even arrived at the pickup spot inside the seedy multi-level parking garage on New Jersey Avenue, a short but starkly contrasting stroll from the bright lights of Bay Boulevard and the heart of Somers Point's tourist district. Arming yourself with guns and sharp knives will do that to a junkie. As will the tantalising promise of fresh drugs.

"What the fuck do you guys want?" said a hooded man with a thick Brooklyn accent. He stood behind a large concrete pillar, cracked and stained with numerous shades of automobile paint, using the shadow to mask his face. In the darkness, a flashy silver watch on his left wrist was his only distinguishing feature.

"I'm here for the drugs," said Hank, rasping to make his voice sound extra menacing in the isolated parking garage. He figured his intentions would be immediately obvious; the baggy black hoody he was wearing couldn't fully hide his gaunt, rake-like appearance, his mottled, pock-marked skin, or his missing front teeth.

"Yeah, we're here for drugs," echoed Hank's friend Mike Rossi, whose sunken skeleton face and red facial sores also betrayed a heavy addiction to methamphetamine. He scratched and swatted at invisible ants on his skin and baggy nondescript clothing as the effects of withdrawal continued to intensify since coming down from his last crystal-meth rush yesterday evening.

"You fools got any money?" said the dealer, sounding doubtful from behind his crumbling concrete shield. "I'm holding, but only if you've got the cheese. Do you know what I mean?"

"No," said Hank, one hand slowly reaching around to the pistol in his back pocket. "We don't."

"Then what the fuck do you expect from me? A freebie? Move the fuck along, white boy. And don't even think about pulling that thing out of your back pocket."

The dealer stepped out from the concrete pillar with his own gun trained firmly on Hank. He pulled back his hood with his other hand, exposing a swarthy complexion, steely brown eyes and a rigid, determined jaw, set beneath a clean-shaven scalp. He looked everything that the two junkies standing in front him were not; strong, fit, healthy, powerful.

But that power drained out of him like noxious smoke from a broken crack pipe when he felt cold steel pressed into the base of his skull. "Don't fucking move," said the man wielding the weapon behind him.

"What the fuck?" The dealer immediately threw his hands in the air, dropping his firearm onto the ground with a loud clang. The noise bounced around the half-empty carpark, ricocheting off concrete pillars and parked cars.

"Good work, Davy," Hank said with a toothless grin, looking around to make sure no-one was watching. "Now shoot his fucking head off, or I will." He removed the pistol from his back pocket and brandished it in front of the dealer. "He's seen our faces now. We can't have this fucker coming after us."

"Yeah, do it," echoed Mike, once again demonstrating a penchant for original thought while he continued to scratch away the imaginary crank bugs that plagued him. "Shoot him, D."

With sallow skin and even sallower teeth, the junkie named Davy Penrose completed the filthy trio of grotesque drug-addled skeletons that were just stupid and desperate enough to rob their dealer at gunpoint. His decay wasn't yet as pronounced as his accomplices', due to being nearly ten years younger. He was just 25 and hadn't been rendered into a skeleton quite yet. Though it would be just a matter of time. In the meantime, he was the only one even remotely capable of wrestling with the drug dealer if their plan to distract him from the front while someone snuck up on him from behind failed.

"Please don't shoot me." The dealer's voice had grown high and screechy, all pretence of being a hardened criminal washed away in the face of probable death. "Please... take the crystal... I'll give you my watch..."

As the dealer went to remove the flashy Rolex from his wrist, Davy pulled the trigger, spraying blood and brain matter all over his two accomplices.

Though the gunshot was heard by several passers-by, the dealer's body wouldn't be discovered until several hours later, lying face-down and watch-less in a large puddle of drying crimson. By then, Hank, Mike, and Davy had smoked up half a bag of the dead drug dealer's crystal meth in the vacant building they squatted in nearby. Paranoid and hungry, their consciousness' expanded and bodies free from the cruel effects of chemical withdrawal, they wiped themselves clean of blood with old newspaper, before making yet another ill-fated decision that would inevitably end in bloodshed.

"What if they come looking for us?" asked Mike, finally rid of the withdrawal-induced invisible insects that had been harassing him since early this morning. He crumpled some bloody newspaper into a ball and attempted to throw it across the room. It flew through a large spider's web before landing in the middle of the dusty, dilapidated floor, which was warped and buckled with age.

Hank was sitting on a flattened cardboard box in the corner, admiring his new Rolex in the glow of the streetlight, which shined through their filthy second-story window. "There's the Mikey we all know and love. Welcome back, buddy. It's good to see you again," he said.

Though he was coherent again, Mike was in no mood for condescension. "I mean it, Hank. The dealer we killed could have been in a gang or something. They could be hunting us down right fucking now, looking for their suitcase full of dope. We don't know. They could sneak in here and kill us in our sleep."

Davy was lying on his cardboard bed in the opposite corner, staring at the roof. "You know, he might have a point, Hank. What if they come after us? Huh? There's only three of us. We've got guns. But what if there's more of them, and they've got guns too? This place isn't big enough to hide us for long."

Hank pulled himself away from admiring his shiny new watch to address his paranoid junky followers. A disgraced army lieutenant in a former life, leadership of the crew was something that had occurred naturally since they'd bandied together a number of months ago. Davy and Mike were already residents of a rat's nest up the coast in Atlantic City when Hank, the oldest and cleverest of the three, stumbled upon it. Under threats of bloody violence, they had quickly yielded whatever dignity and methamphetamine they still possessed to Hank, and the trio had been together ever since, hustling for money up and down the Jersey Shore and getting high whenever possible. "Okay, okay, you babies," he said. "I hear you loud and clear. We'll lay low for a while."

That wasn't enough reassurance for Mike, who continued to pace back and forth through the dust and rat shit that littered the old wooden floor. "What if they come looking for us here? I mean, half the druggies and dealers in Jersey probably already know who we are. Someone easily could have followed us. I say we take the suitcase and get out of here, before they find us and end us."

Hank climbed to his feet and forcefully stopped Mike's frantic pacing by placing both of his hands on the smaller man's shoulders. "Relax. Even if that dealer does have connections, no-one knows we were there."

"But what if...?"

Hank slapped Mike hard across the face. "I told you to relax. Now sit down." He shoved the skinny junkie onto the flattened cardboard box that he used for a bed. "Both of you, listen up. I hear your concerns, and I assure you that they're unfounded. They'd probably be here already if they were coming to get us."

He paused for a long moment, giving his worn and weary synapses a chance to fire. Mike stared up at him from his prone position on the filthy cardboard, while Davy continued to stare at the cobwebbed ceiling, still riding the pale-white dragon through the night sky above Somers Point, only half aware of the events where his physical form lay, malnourished and prematurely decaying.

Finally, Hank laid out his latest scheme. "To put your drug-addled minds to rest, we'll get out of here tonight, go sleep in JFK park, down by the harbour. It'll be cold as hell, but we won't be as closed in as we are here, so if we see anyone come after us—I know we won't, but *if* we do— we'll be able to get away. Now gather up your shit, and we'll get out of here."

It was a surprisingly coherent and strategically sound plan from the former army man, whose sharp military mind had otherwise been rendered reckless and stupid from years of assaulting his central nervous systems with anything and everything that would get him high.

Over the next hour, these three unwise men packed up their meagre possessions, which largely consisted of torn and tatty clothing, their weapons, and smoking paraphernalia, and trudged their way past yacht clubs and fine-dining restaurants, noisy bars and fancy hotels. As they cut a swath through throngs of tourists, dragging a characterless black suitcase full of methamphetamine in their wake, these emaciated skeletons barely warranted a glance from the general populace for fear that they might be asked if they could spare a few bucks.

Meanwhile, across the city and a world away, Billy and his friends were cruising down Ocean Heights Avenue in a late-model SUV, blithely unaware that that they were on a collision course with a trio of paranoid junkies armed with guns.

When the shooting started, they were going to wish they had stayed home to study like good boys.

3

Though it was an unseasonably warm night, summer had long come and gone in this part of the world, taking much of John F Kennedy Park's greenery with it. The naked trees' moonlit silhouettes only added to the Halloween fun, with a big-screen hidden amongst a skeletal copse near the park's rear, the blackened Atlantic Ocean as its backdrop. As hundreds of scary-movie fans bought snacks from mobile food vendors and took their seats, a trio of junkies, and a quintet of young people carrying clown masks in their backpacks, entered the park from opposite ends. They were destined to meet somewhere near the middle when the film finally began.

Hank, Mike, and Davy carefully wheeled their suitcase full of drugs through the park, keeping their paranoid eyes open for police, or vengeful drug dealers looking to recoup their losses—a fool's errand in the failing light. In the moonlight and under the park's lamps, everyone looked malign, threatening, ominous. No-one looked harmless, even though many of the people at the park that night were young teenagers, seeking a safe thrill on Halloween night.

They'd get a thrill alright, but it would be far from a safe night out among the stars and the trees. Hank and his lackeys all-but guaranteed as much when they decided to smoke some more of their ill-gotten gains within sight of the pop-up cinema.

Davy sparked his crack pipe and inhaled the pernicious white smoke. He held it in for as long as he could, before blowing a smoke stream up into the moonlight. "What do you reckon they're doing over there?" he asked, pointing at the crowd. His mind began to float away.

"Looks like some sort of gathering," said Mike, exhaling slowly, his eyes already rolling back into their sockets.

Hank's eyes rolled in his head—not only from methamphetamine-induced euphoria, but also in exasperation. "Very observant, Einstein. Of course, it's a ruddy gathering. Looks like some sort of a movie night to me."

"Good guess," agreed Davy, his voice wan and haggard from trying to keep the smoke in his lungs and talk at the same time. When he couldn't hold it in any longer, he began to cough and pound his chest with his free hand, hacking out the smoke into the mild night air.

"Damned right it is. I'm not the brains around here for nothing. We'll go sit in the back when you boys have finished up here. Just don't go getting catatonic on me just yet. I'll leave you both behind if you do." Hank snatched Mike's pipe out of his hands and refilled it. A short time later, he also tweaked in the moonlight.

Meanwhile, Billy Mills and his four pals spread out amongst the jacketed cinema-goers, strategically taking seats on all four sides of the congregation, so that they could don their masks and frighten the audience at the designated time, effectively boxing in their would-be victims. Intoxicated with giddy anticipation, as well as copious amounts of alcohol, they waited nervously for the film to begin, backpacks at their feet.

All lights but those that marked the exits went out as the movie began to play.

Shrill piano notes silenced all in attendance. They repeated from the surrounding sound system, echoing around the audience, gradually building in intensity. Then synth chords stabbed the melody like a knife as the opening credits played on the big screen next to a sinister glowing pumpkin, carved into a sinister face. When John Carpenter's name came on the screen, the crowd found its voice again. Everyone cheered and applauded for a full minute, before a simple white title card on a black background silenced them once more. You could practically hear a pin drop as the audience was transported to Haddonfield, Illinois, on Halloween night in 1963.

As the audience experienced that cool autumn evening through young Michael Myers' eyes, their own pupils and retinas were focussed so intently on the big screen that no-one noticed when Billy and his friends began to put on their rubber clown masks and remove sharp-looking machetes and knives from their backpacks. The tension soared to nearly overwhelming levels, not just for the audience watching Myers stalk his family home, but the killer clowns too, as they grinned in the darkness, waiting for the opportune moment to strike.

That moment came approximately four minutes later. Michael, having ruthlessly dispatched his sister in the opening scene, is unmasked by his parents, who are still unaware of the chaos inside their idyllic family home—just as the people watching were also unaware of the chaos that was about to unfold around them.

Naturally, Billy led the charge. He jumped up from his seat and loudly laughed like a maniac, his cackling distracting almost everyone from the twist in the movie which would have been so shocking back in 1978. He plunged his knife into the woman sitting next to him, hurting her with its sharp point, but not mortally wounding her or even piercing her skin because his utensil was made of cheap plastic, not sharpened steel. She screamed anyway, ostensibly making the knife seem real to all the people watching on, and in the ensuing panic, Billy's friends also made their presences known.

Following their ringleader's example, four more killer clowns popped up like sinister jack-in-the-boxes on all sides of the audience, laughing, stabbing, thrusting their fake knives into people while the movie continued to play, now totally unwatched by its frightened audience. Like panicked cattle, most of the crowd scattered towards the exits, pushing and shoving each other, knocking over seats in desperation to get away.

Witnessing the chaos from the back row of the pop-up movie theatre, paranoid junkie Mike opened fire into the crowd. Though his intentions were almost heroic—to kill the evil clowns before they could kill everyone else—his body and mind were deeply under the influence of narcotics, so he did not pause to consider the possibility that this was anything other than real, or that he might miss. He aimed for the clown closest to him and killed a different man when his stray shot penetrated his cerebrum, murdering the father of two instantly. More stray bullets ripped into other moviegoers' arms, legs, and torsos, before a shot finally found its designated target.

Nate Smith—simply "Smithy" to his friends—was shot in the stomach.

One moment he was waving a plastic machete at terrified teens, the next he was haemorrhaging gore on the ground, terrified and in agony, his whimpers for help suppressed by the screams erupting all around the park. Before he succumbed to death, his staunchly Catholic parents like to think their wayward son prayed for absolution, but the only thing on Smithy's mind in his last-ever moments of consciousness was blind panic as the junkie who just shot him walked over to where he lay, raised his gun and prepared to shoot.

Before Mike could pull the trigger, another clown tackled him, knocking the scrawny junkie sideways. The man in the mask was Steve Simpson, an English major at Somers Point Community College and a friend of Smithy's since high school. The junkie and the clown crashed into the grass together, where they rolled amongst the chaos of panicked moviegoers, entangling themselves—Mike trying to get a shot away, and Steve trying to wrestle away the gun.

The clown inevitably won. The long-time drug addict's battered body was never going to be a match for youth and a protein-rich diet. A determined Steve finally wrenched the pistol away from a panting Mike, and, before the junkie could catch his breath, the younger man fired a single shot into Mike's right eye, ending him, and removing a sizeable chunk of his skull in the process. Blood splattered all over the clown mask, staining its grinning white teeth crimson.

As Steve slowly got back to his feet, Hank strode up behind him, shoved his gun into the back of the clown's head, and tore it open with a bullet to the brain.

An onlooker screamed in the moonlight. The same person would later tell police that the killer clown had it coming. The men with guns had saved them from a "gang of killer clowns" that were "hellbent on slaughtering as many people as they possibly could". Fox News would lead its breaking news update with these quotes. They would subsequently be plastered across headlines worldwide, before the true facts of the case finally came to light several days later.

But while it's most likely true that Mike and Davy thought the killer-clown threat was real, it's debatable whether the wily old army lieutenant felt the same way. For him, the chaos was likely just an excuse to act on his psychopathic urges, and to re-live his combat glory days. He'd served in Kosovo and Bosnia in the 1990s, before he was handed a dishonourable discharge due to fledgling drug dependency issues that would worsen during the following decades, eventually resulting in a life on the streets of New Jersey.

Before his first kill of the evening had hit the ground, Hank was already hunting the next. Though the crowd had thinned out, a throng of people still gathered between two mobile food stalls—now vacant—which had jammed them in a slowly moving bottleneck. Menacing the crowd was an overweight clown named Derek Lawrence, a Philosophy major who should have been at home studying for an examination the next day, a test that he would never get the opportunity to sit.

As Derek brandished a butcher's knife, he bellowed desperately unfunny insults to the frightened masses frantically trying to leave, which might be why he didn't join them when the shooting began. He simply didn't hear the gunshots over all the screaming and the sound of his own voice. It's also why he didn't know Hank was creeping up behind him until it was too late. "Hey, fuck you!" Derek screamed in one man's face. "You're ugly!" he shouted to the man's wife. "You are a piece of shit!" he yelled to their young daughter.

"No, you are," said Hank, cutting off Derek's hateful tirade and shooting the fat clown in the face.

When the clown attack began, Hank left Davy in charge of protecting their suitcase full of dope while he and Mike went off to make a bad situation even worse. Now Mike was dead, along with three of the five clowns, and still Davy stayed put, a silent, wild-eyed witness to the deadly chaos that had embroiled the park. As police sirens eventually began to ring out in the distance, he finally decided to move the merchandise to safety.

The junkie trudged along familiar ground, back to where he and his friends had smoked some crack just over half an hour and several bloody murders ago.

Along the way, he wheeled the suitcase past people who were either too injured or too frightened to get away. Some of them whimpered for help, others were silent, all of them wore thousand-yard stares as more screams rang out across the park and the movie continued to play on the big screen. The first dead clown, Nate Smith, lay face-down in the dirt, a pool of blood slowly expanding around his midsection. Though he didn't know it, Davy also walked within a couple of yards of where his former friend Mike lay, his drug-addled brain still seeping out onto the lush green lawn.

Davy stumbled upon the two remaining clowns nearby, both of them holding savage-looking knives behind an old oak tree. Though they had their backs to him, the dope fiend could see the edges of their sinister red smiles in the moonlight.

Davy whipped out his gun. "Don't fucking move," he said, unwittingly repeating his line from earlier in the evening. "I'll fucking shoot you both where you stand. Now drop those fucking knives before I put a fucking bullet in your heads."

They dropped them. "They're not real knives anyway," said the clown that was really Jamie Walsh in disguise. His voice was muffled under a layer of latex.

"What the fuck did you say?"

Jamie removed his mask so that the man holding the gun could hear him better. "I said the knives aren't real. None of it is. It's all bullshit. You get it? We were just clowning." His voice wavered, on the verge of tears. "It's a prank, a bad joke gone horribly, horribly wrong."

That was an understatement.

Shocked that the killer clown had a human face, Davy lowered his weapon while his drug-addled mind struggled to make sense of everything. Were they really just young people in Halloween costumes, scaring everyone as part of some sick joke? Surely no-one could be so fucking stupid...

His train of thought was interrupted by Hank, who was marching towards him from the direction of the pop-up movie theatre, his gun in one hand and a fake machete in the other. "Davy, what are you doing over there? You better not have lost our suitcase or I'm going to kill you, son. I mean it, son. You will die."

Davy waved to him. "Hank, I've captured two of the clowns. They say..."

The suitcase crashed down on Davy's skull, and he collapsed to the ground with it, spilling the gun, and a large amount of blood from a severe gash on his pock-marked forehead.

"Davy?" Hank began to run towards the tree, while from behind it, Billy stooped to pick up the gun.

"What the fuck are you doing?" asked Jamie, pulling his clown mask back down to hide his face. "You're going to get us killed."

"Not unless I kill this fucker first," said Billy, clutching the gun in both hands, his back against the tree's trunk, waiting for Hank to appear. "Get back against the tree. He's going to see you in a second."

Hank already had. Shooting from a kneeling position, the former military man managed to pierce Jamie's throat from 75 yards. The sound of the shot ricocheted off the tree, but the bullet did not; it buried itself deep in the trunk. Though Hank was aiming for Jamie's head, he was more than satisfied when his quarry clutched at his throat, trying to stem the tide of blood surging onto the ground.

As the clown toppled over, Hank blasted another shot into the tree, which served as a warning to the last remaining clown that he knew was hiding behind it.

Billy gritted his teeth and waited patiently, trying hard to concentrate on the sound of the approaching junkie and not on his friend dying noisily in the dirt beside him, his pierced throat gurgling as oxygen and blood mixed. "Get the fuck out of here," his friend said up to him through a mouthful of blood. "Go, run."

Billy did not run.

Nor was Hank foolish enough to move within sight of the last remaining clown.

Both men merely stood their ground, saying nothing, waiting, watching, listening intently, while police sirens grew louder and Jamie finally gurgled his last strangled breath on the ground.

The police had finally arrived.

4

During his 30 years with the Somers Point Police Department, officer George Lomax only had to unholster his weapon once—to prevent a group of white supremacists from beating a young black man to death outside of the Applebee's on Jackson Street in 2009—and he was fortunate to have never needed to fire it in the line of duty.

It was a point of pride for the veteran law enforcer, who's roly-poly appearance and bright-white beard automatically marked him as the department's Santa Claus for the past seven Christmases in a row. The man known affectionately as 'Kringle' had seen so very many horrible things while performing his duty over the years, but he had never once lost faith in the fundamental goodness of humanity, even as he arrested drug dealers and murderers, robbers and rapists, wife beaters and paedophiles.

The carnage that welcomed him when he was the first officer on the scene in John F Kennedy Park would challenge that notion more than anything before, and eventually break it beyond repair.

As his squad car sped down John F Kennedy Park Drive—normally so idyllic during the day time, but hellish that October evening—he passed flocks of frightened cinemagoers, all lit blue-and-red in the flashing lights on top of the vehicle. They waved frantically at him, screaming about gunmen and killer clowns. Though it pained him to not stop and offer them comfort, he felt he could not spare a single moment; he needed to ascertain the situation with his own eyes first, and then radio back for support if needed.

He parked by the playground and walked to the pop-up cinema with his hand on the handle of his pistol, his radio chirruping away on his belt. He could hear yelling in the distance, the words distorted by distance and ambient park noise, but the only screams he could hear were coming from the film.

He found the bodies of Mike Rossi and Steve Simpson first, both with sizeable chunks missing from their heads. He did not need to check for a pulse, because there was no point; still-fresh blood and brain matter abounded on the grassy ground, especially out the back of the younger man's head, which appeared to have been obliterated by a single bullet fired at point-blank range.

That's when George drew his firearm for only the second time in his policing career.

Inside the pop-up cinema, he found more than a dozen people cowering beneath mobile food vendors and fold-up seats while the movie continued to play above them. A white-masked man in overalls was terrorising a young Jamie Lee Curtis, who was taking refuge in a closet. George had never been much of a fan of the genre, having had more than his fill of horror during his long police career. He looked away from the big screen and could see right away that several people were severely injured. He resisted the urge to rush over and offer them assistance. He told himself that they looked as though they would live—not like the civilian sprawled on the ground next to a weeping woman, presumably his wife.

She continued to bawl as the old officer leaned over to check the man's pulse, feeling nothing. His own heart sunk in his chest.

Saying nothing, George kept his gun ready as he moved on to what appeared to be a young man in a clown mask, lying on his back in a pool of his own blood. The clown did not move as George knelt on the soft ground beside him. He lifted the mask back an inch and pressed his index and middle fingers into the soft hollow area beside the man's windpipe.

The clown was completely still, cold, dead.

That's when George radioed for backup. "Multiple homicides in John F Kennedy Park," he said, finding the calmness in his own voice shocking given how he far from calm he was feeling at that moment, easily the scariest in his entire life. "I repeat, there have been multiple homicides in JFK Park. Requesting immediate backup, and please send an ambulance if you haven't already. There looks to be about a dozen severely injured persons. Maybe more. Over."

"Copy," the radio hissed back at him. "Police and ambulance are on the way. Over."

"Roger that. I'm going to secure the scene now. Over and out."

George's old joints creaked and cracked as he stood up from his kneeling position. His radio squawked on his hip once more, causing his heart to lurch in his chest. He pivoted, finger on the trigger of his gun, checking for assailants. Seeing none, he calmed himself with three deep breaths, before switching off his radio to prevent further frights. The old officer had never had a heart attack before this night, and he gravely wanted to keep it that way.

He proceeded to walk around the periphery of chairs, many of which had been tipped over and thrown about in people's desperation to leave. The lights of a fried food stand continued to glow, but no-one stood behind the register. Someone's order of hamburger and fries sat there, going cold and unwanted on the stainless-steel counter. Insects buzzed around the food and in the moonlight in general. Besides their constant drone, the soft whimpering of one of the victim's, and the movie, there were no other sounds.

The police officer walked back over to where several victims were taking shelter beneath a caravan that sold Mexican food, before it was vacated when the shooting began. "Stay put," he whispered to a man trying in vain to stifle the crimson flowing from a wound in his stomach. "Help is on its way."

"Please don't go," the man said through gritted teeth.

"I have to," said George, already turning away. "You just keep holding on. More help is on the way"

George left the pop-up cinema a few minutes later. Still carrying his gun with two hands in front of him, he walked along a poorly lit concrete footpath, listening out for gun shots or screams and hearing none, constantly checking for anyone hiding amongst the skeletal trees that flanked the path and seeing none. He could hear sirens coming somewhere in the distance, which filled his heart with hope, even as he worried that they would not get to the park in time.

His fears proved prophetic when he stumbled across a scene from out of a coulrophobic nightmare. Next to an old oak tree, two bloodied bodies lay on the ground, motionless. A person in a sinister-looking clown mask stood over them, holding a firearm in his hands.

Adrenaline pumping, heart pounding in his ears, the veteran policeman addressed the perp who was standing side-on to the tree. "Hey, you there, drop your gun, or I'll have to shoot you! This is your only warning!"

As Billy whirled around to face the policeman, Davy stirred on the ground, his head aching from having a suitcase full of meth crash into it. He tried to speak and discovered that he couldn't. His throat was dry, his brain was numb. Disorientated, the scraggy drug addict tried to stand, stumbled, and collapsed back down hard in the dirt.

Hearing the noise, Billy swivelled back around and, without a moment's hesitation, shot Davy at close range in the chest, ensuring the youngest of the trio of meth addicts would never get high ever again.

Almost as quickly, the muzzle of George's gun flared in the moonlight. The old police officer pulled the trigger on his Sig Sauer P229 three times: the first shot grazed Billy's shoulder before getting lodged in the tree; the second pierced nothing but air; the third and final shot, which was fired a mere second after the first, found its designated target.

Billy's forehead burst open like an overripe melon that had been dropped from a great height, instantly ending the young man's life, as well as the career of the policeman who fired the fatal shot.

George would hand in his notice the following day. Although he would undergo years of therapy at the tax payer's expense, he would never get that image of a clown's head exploding out of his mind. Over and over again, it would play in his brain whenever he closed his eyes, and sometimes even when they were open. He would never be the same again. No-one who had been at the park that night would be.

At least Billy and his friends were spared the ignominy of what happened in the immediate fall-out from the event in John F Kennedy Park when police were still under the false impression that the suitcase of methamphetamine recovered at the crime scene was theirs. A fingerprint test, which led to Hank's subsequent apprehension and conviction, as well as a testimonial from multiple eyewitnesses who swore that they saw one of the dead junkies wheeling a suitcase in the lead-up to the shooting cleared their names of that charge posthumously, but not before the media ran wild with stories of drug-dealing killer clowns.

The bloody episode was quickly dubbed "The Killer Clown Massacre", a name that has lived on in infamy, despite the vehement protests of the friends and relatives of the clowns in question. They argued that their children, brothers, classmates and friends were the true victims that Halloween, not only of the country's ever-growing methamphetamine problem, but also of a mass media that had glamorised the great clown panic in the first place.

Suddenly nobody thought it was funny or cool to dress up as a clown to scare people any more.

Simon Petersen's first novel, *Slasher Sam*, was released in 2017.

When he's not writing, you can find him on Twitter @bysimonpetersen where he spouts nonsense about craft beer, sport, travel, and his favourite subject of them all: horror.

Beneath Black Balloons

Jeremy Megargee

The mirror is an abyss, and it keeps looking back at me. Fractured, but not the glass. The fracture is in my head. Fragments, shrapnel, pieces of jagged thoughts. They're sharp, and they always cut, and it leaves me lost and lacerated. Do you ever see your own reflection, and the first impulse is to scream? No? Can't relate? Welcome to the life of Caliban the Clown. I see myself, this bulging face, these sagging jowls, these bloodshot eyeballs, the shriveled arms, the flabby belly, the wiry body hair, and all of it boils in the brain, it becomes a grotesquerie, and I can't escape it, I can't embrace it, there's literally nothing I can do but stare and hate, stare and hate, stare and hate...

I'm intimate with the feeling of self-hatred. She's an old lover, and her tongue is made of razorblades. She's always kissing me, and I'm always trying to push her away, but she's aggressive, she's abusive, and the word "no" never sinks in. I want to love myself, but when I'm smearing on lipstick and powdering oily cheeks, I often wonder, is there anything in me that deserves it?

Beneath Black Balloons

He's running late, stumbling in the mud with floppy pink shoes. The magenta wig is lank with the rain, and faux hair plasters against his brow. The insomniac within gave him hell last night, and he botched the order, and now all that he brings is a handful of black balloons. He wanted them to be lively, colorful, helium-globes to make the kids laugh and smile. Will the children see the black, those ugly black balloons, and think him ugly too? Will they laugh at his comedic routines and his silent mime dance, or will they laugh at the man beneath the greasepaint? The broken, bloodless man that he is...

The toe of his shoe catches on the roots of a dead oak, and he goes down into the grass. He comes up splattered in the darkest of dirt, and through a mask of grime, he sees that the park is empty. The birthday party canceled, and no one bothered to contact the clown. A gloved hand releases multiple strings, and bloated black balloons float off into an overcast sky that has no choice but to take them.

The pills jingle in their bottles as I open the medicine cabinet, and then the mirror is back, and it frowns at me, a soul-frown, and you can't fix that. Those useless medications, the ones that dull, giving only fog, and I know deep down that I can't suppress what's inside. The quacks keep telling me it's body dysmorphic disorder. They judge from behind clipboards, looking down on me from narrowed and spectacled eyes. There's nothing physically wrong with you, Caliban the Clown. You're normal, ordinary, and what you see are exaggerated flaws, and you must learn to see past them. It's like telling an elephant to look past his trunk. Explain to the porcupine that he doesn't have quills. Whisper to the monster, tell him he's a model, and the whole wide world snickers in the dark. I smell their lies, and each one is like shit packed up into my nostrils to the point where it nauseates me.

I become physically ill at the sight of my reflection.

I want to scrape out the contents of my stomach until it's all clean again, but I know that a thing like me was born to be dirty, bred to crawl in filth, and the disintegration of self is not imagined, but a harsh reality. I tap broken fingernails against the glass, and wouldn't it be sweet to reach through, rip off that big red nose, stuff it down the throat, and choke? Choke forever, and each gurgle brings me closer to the blackness, only black, like pitch black balloons...

I scrub my hands against my own shaved skull, the fissured scars along my wrists and forearms seeming especially noticeable in the bathroom fluorescents.

I can't count how many times I've tried to cut out the pain, catch it at the root, but it's planted too deep, and it *always* grows back.

———

The rusty Ferris wheel creaks in the wind, and emaciated lions pace behind iron bars, gnawing at bones with precious little meat to be found on them. There's no life in the eyes of the lions. No shine, no wildness. Born in cages, the sunlight and the soil as foreign to them as the concept of hunting for sustenance. Caliban's tent is close to their enclosure, and looking at them for too long deadens his heart. The rubes come and go, playing rigged games, chuckling with carnies who desire only to part cash from their wallets. The kids love the rides, old and outdated as they are, and many a small face can be found stuffing funnel cakes and cotton candy into the mouth.

The carnival is alive with people, but Caliban feels alone in the crowd. His tent is rarely visited. It leaves him as deflated as the balloon animals that he tries his best to twist into unnatural existence. His smile is forced, and somehow they know it, sense it, and as a result the people avoid him on a primordial level.

The comments come with the wind, and each one is a barb to his ears. These are children of a modern age, raised on video game consoles, tablets, and the instant gratification of a smartphone app. They have words to describe a clown like him. Lame. Boring. Dumb.

The words build up in his head, and a frown etches itself onto Caliban's face. It's deep-set and grooved, furrows in the flesh, an inversion of a rictus, and even the paint can't hide the misery. His eyes are hollow, tormented, and comparable to the pianist who finally realizes that his hands are broken, and they have been broken all along.

It's this damn festering right arm that's the worst. It's disproportionate, I just know it. It's longer than the other arm. The fingers are a quarter of an inch lower than the fingers on the left hand. It's not fair. An abominable deformity, and maybe that's all they see when I'm dancing and honking and pantomiming for them...

The scissors? No. They scrape the skin, but not enough. The wire brush? It brings the blood blisters, like lancing off cancerous parts of the soul, but it can't fucking fix me. I need a release. It's too much pressure. Clowning around about the town, but who likes the clown with the frown? I'd be happier if it was gone. Those fingers are five separate betrayals. The bony wrist is a Judas Iscariot in the sacred grove that is my body. That forearm—misshapen, bent, hanging like sour meat, *mocking* me—

I loathe it, it's everything that's wrong with my life, my failures, my imperfections, it can't be part of me, it doesn't *fit* with the rest.

Well I glutted myself on that t-bone earlier, didn't I? More yellowish fat to pad out the insides. There's the cutting board out in the kitchen. And that old pitted cleaver, the one I got at the flea market last year...

A face in the mirror, all blurry with tears, and streaks running down the crackling greasepaint. It's my own godforsaken visage, and why can't the muscles in my face form a proper smile?!?

Cleave, clown.

Cleave until the frown goes upside down.

————————

The porcelain sink is marred with scarlet inkblots, the flow like warm molasses down the drain. The cleaver has been abandoned in the toilet, the blade chipped from the act of hacking. The only sound in the tiny bathroom is a slow drip, but it's not water that drips. Caliban the Clown is the source of the leak.

He stares at himself in the mirror. For the first time in a long time, there's genuine mirth gleaming in those forlorn eyes. A sense of purpose. A renewed sense of self, and life unfolds to him like the open canvas of a cosmic carnival tent.

He brings up his right hand to paint his lips, but that hand is gone, hacked to the bone, and the stump remaining terminates just below the forearm. The flesh is inflamed, spurting rosy red color, and the white of the jutting bone matches the pallor of Caliban's face. He smiles, the greasepaint flaking from his cheeks, and it's the expression of a man who has found peace inside of himself.

He uses that little shard of blood-speckled bone like a tube of lipstick, and he smears a big red grin onto his face to go along with the big red nose and the big red bloodshot eyes. He paints until it's perfect. Until he is perfect. Caliban the Clown offers the mirror a convincing crimson grin, and he leaves the saturated glass behind as he wobbles to the door.

He dances while he bleeds, eager for a final performance.

Jeremy Megargee has always loved dark fiction. He cut his teeth on R.L Stine's Goosebumps series as a child and a fascination with Stephen King's work followed later in life. Jeremy weaves his tales of personal horror from Martinsburg, West Virginia with his cat Lazarus acting as his muse/familiar.

Follow his work at www.facebook.com/JMHorrorFiction

Email: TheDeadEngine@yahoo.com

I, Clown

Robert Morgan Fisher

He ran away and joined the circus. But that's never how it goes. The circus came to town and he let it take him. The reasons why aren't important. Bad grades, bad family, bad feelings. The circus gave good feelings when it swung through town each summer. He liked everything about it: the food, freaks, animals...

Clowns.

Those clowns. So funny, so happy. A trip to the circus was always thrilling. First with his parents, then later—after they split up—with his friends. They'd roam the midway, smoking, discreetly pulling from a pint in a paper bag. That fascination with clowns' greasepaint, gags, timing. He never lost it. Always wanted to be a clown. That was the job for him. No idea how to go about it other than hiring on with a circus and agreeing to do anything.

Anything.

Just take me with you.

He approached some clowns on a smoke break by their trailer, in what circus folk call Clown Alley. They were holy men to him. Offstage, they looked deactivated, low-key and more human.

I, Clown

Wanna be a clown, he said.

Go see the Ring Master, they said. Good luck.

They laughed, suddenly looking again like real clowns.

Ring Master hired him to clean animal cages. Feeding and watering too. Hard work but he did a good job. When they packed up and left town, he went along, but had to travel and sleep with the animals.

He kept after those clowns. Show me the ropes, he insisted. One agreed to teach him. He became a clown apprentice. Ring Master approved of this only if he continued to take care of the animals, which he did. He liked animals and was never mean to them. Moved a lot of poop, he did. Lots of hay, feed, water. Always hosing out cages, stalls. He smelled like an animal but it didn't keep girls away. He'd get lucky sometimes, letting some girl from town see the animals up close.

He understood that he was no Don Juan—they were seduced by the circus, as he had been.

One of the few things he'd brought along with him when he ran away was an ancient book on clowning. It was very wholesome, published by some church-run company. But it contained the total how-to on being a clown or, as it was sometimes referred to, jesting. Clowns had a long, fabled history; the word Clown derived from the word "clod" which, he noted (with amused self-satisfaction) rhymed with "odd" and "god."

Soon he became a full-time clown. They hired some other kid they picked up along the way to tend the animals. He bunked with the clowns and was initiated into their various practices and rituals. He created his own special clown face: Auguste exaggerated features, white around the mouth, ruddy pink base, big red nose, squirting flower, tiny hat. The big shoes, of course.

Though he studied his clown-book, he'd never been book smart. He made up for it with lean body-strength, flexibility and something approaching grace. They had their own book of routines which he devoured and mastered: Yes, No Banana; Say Ouch; Henpecked Henry. This went on for several years under the big top with the Ring Master, one elephant, two lions, a few monkeys and a husband & wife high-wire-trapeze team. A regular circus family.

The clowns entered the big top and exited in a little clown car which was actually, underneath, an ancient golf cart.

He never tired of it.

One day, a well-dressed man approached him on his way back to Clown Alley. The man asked a few questions, including how much he was currently making. The man said he was staying in town at a hotel and gave him his card. Call me there, he said. As the man walked away, he read the card and almost fainted. The man was from the colossal circus—you know the one. His job was to poach clown talent from smaller operations.

After thinking it over, he called and made an appointment with the man.

Should I wear my greasepaint? he asked.

No, said the man, I've seen it.

He showed up at the hotel feeling a little exposed without his red nose and tiny hat. They met in the bar. The man bought him an expensive dinner and drinks. The big circus was owned by a corporation. There was an actual clown college—which had recently closed down. So now they had to recruit from smaller circuses.

He told the man he felt was like he was being called up to the majors.

I, Clown

Only when you're called up to *our* show, the man said, there's an actual *show*.

Then the man laughed and lit a cigar.

Don't worry, he said, it won't explode.

By the end of the week, he gave notice. The other clowns took it hard. Some were jealous, but most wished him luck, compelled by the sacred bonds of their profession.

––––––––––

The colossal circus was a mixed bag—mostly good. Food was better, private trailer. They put his face on a poster. That was a big deal. He couldn't believe this was his life now. He soon grew comfortable with it. Never complacent—but less anxious. He had a little money, was treated well and got to do what he loved.

Sometimes, after a long day of clowning or traveling, he'd read from his clown book. The big circus had its own clown book—they all do—but he still enjoyed flipping through the simple routines, savoring the cartoon illustrations. Classic clown-craft. It reminded him of how far he'd come.

When they came to a town, the clowns often visited sick kids in the hospital. He loved doing that. The bald kids on chemo were his favorite. They just lit up when the clowns entered the ward.

Every time they left, he'd sit down in his seat on the bus, turn to his fellow circus folk and say: I clown—and I cure cancer.

They'd solemnly smile and nod. They all believed it.

––––––––––

He saved a little money—not much, but enough. He never married, never found the right girl—that is, one who liked to live in a trailer. Sometimes he wished he had kids of his own, but then they'd drive into the ring in their little clown car and he had all the kid-love he could handle.

But then, things began to change. Attendance began to fall off. The circus wasn't as popular as it once was. The animal rights people were on the warpath. To be fair, lions, monkeys and elephants would probably be happier in the wild—but they were well-cared for in this famous circus. It was a point of pride. Even in the smaller circus, the animals had been treated well. But the animal rights people were determined to change things—maybe for the best.

The other thing was that clowns began to fall out of favor. First, they became popular villains in movies. This wasn't hard to understand; part of a clown's appeal is that he's—well, a little creepy. He knew that. That was the beauty of it. Like a sexy woman in a cop uniform—we're a little in love with what scares us.

But this was a whole different development. Movie clowns now epitomized evil. Audiences ate it up. They expected clowns to torture, slaughter, dismember. Some of them specialized in murdering kids—which broke his heart.

The other thing was when a serial killer turned out to have worked as a clown? Well, the media just went berserk. Especially if the killer happened to fixate on kids. Then it was open season. It was humiliating and outrageous. Sometimes local TV news reporters would corner him with provocative questions. He'd be there in clown makeup, trying to conceal his rage. He'd wind up looking and sounding like a psycho. It just wasn't fair.

I, Clown

There were cutbacks, layoffs. He was pressured into early retirement. The small severance package wasn't enough to live on, so he had to take the first job he could find, with a carnival.

A carnival is not a circus. It's more like the ghetto of clowning.

The people, carnies, have their own culture, their own language. He was, in fact, the only clown in this particular carnival. His job was to put the scare on people as they rode on a light-rail through the haunted house. Various monsters would pop out of the wall and try to grab you. They made him change his makeup. Using some of the more popular clown-horror movie clichés as a guide, he transformed himself into an angry fiend. It wasn't hard to manufacture the anger part. He acquired fake fangs; gave little or no thought as to how he applied his greasepaint—the sloppier and more psychopathic, the better. Whereas before the greasepaint contained a happy soul, it now restrained bad intent.

Kids had changed. They wanted to be scared, and clowns were the scariest. He considered quitting, maybe become a freelance birthday clown. But those kids were the same kids coming to the carnival and god only knows what that would be like. And he needed the steady, if not meager, carnival paycheck. The carnival pushed him to be more aggressive and sometimes he began to feel a foreign, strange sexual thrill if he made a kid cry—something he knew was completely wrong. He loathed the carnival, his job and himself.

Then one day, he put the scare into this boy and everything went haywire. A split-second before he lunged, he saw something different in the kid's eyes. The boy wasn't just scared, this was true trauma. His parents on either side of him seemed to sense it too. But before he could make an adjustment, the boy jumped out and ran until he found an exit and didn't stop running. The parents tried to catch the boy but couldn't.

He heard that they later found him on the highway a half-mile away, hit by a truck. He was rushed to the hospital and put on life-support.

———

The next morning, he quit the carnival. Though he had no idea where this town was until he looked at a map, he just couldn't go on. He collected his pay and rented a cheap, furnished apartment over a liquor store.

He slept for twelve hours at a time.

He began to drink—something he'd managed to avoid all these years—but it now seemed like a good time to start. He barely ate and when he did it was crap food. He found a small, cruddy TV on someone's sidewalk with a sign on it that said: FREE—WORKS.

He slept, watched TV and drank.

A few months went by.

He tried to remember his old life with the big circus. It seemed like all that had happened on another planet.

———

One day, the local news reported that the boy, who turned out to be autistic, had been taken off life-support but was still in a coma. Doctors were hopeful.

When he heard this, he was sitting, slumped in the ratty easy chair, holding a watery drink in his hand with all the ice melted. He got up, waddled over to the kitchen sink and dumped out the drink. Then he opened the cupboard and emptied all the bottles as well.

He sniffed his armpits and realized he stank.

Showered, shaved, brewed some coffee.

Opened the windows.

Changed the sheets.

Did laundry.

He began to buy actual groceries and cook real meals. He started a regimen of calisthenics and began to regain his old form.

A few weeks later, more news: the boy had come out of his coma. His parents were on TV, thanking everyone for their prayers, cards and good wishes. He didn't recognize their faces from that fateful night—it'd been dark in the haunted house—but in their combined features he could clearly recall the terror-stricken boy.

They thanked the doctors. The kid was still recovering. They said he could now talk and move his legs.

This last bit of news caused him to break down and cry.

When he'd pulled himself together, he got on the phone.

He tracked down the boy's parents. He explained who he was and what this tragedy had done to him. They got his whole life story, how he'd once been a circus performer—not a cheap carnival sellout, but a real honest-to-god clown in the most famous circus of all.

He begged them for a chance to visit the boy—as his old clown self. This was something he was good at, he told them. He'd visited many children in the hospital over the years and was sure this would be a good thing. They were uncertain at first, but finally agreed to meet him at the hospital the next day outside of intensive care.

All night long, he could barely contain his excitement. He visualized everything: the gags, the props, what he'd say. Surely, this would be a healing and happy experience.

In the morning, he got up and readied himself: shave, shower, makeup. He put on his big floppy shoes for the first time in ages. Ditto the squirting flower. He filled it with water, tested it in the bathroom mirror. Popped on his nose and adjusted the tiny hat. He ran downstairs to the liquor store, bought some candy and other items.

It felt so good.

Proudly and merrily, he strode to the hospital, prop bag in hand. People stared in awe, pointing and covering their smiling mouths. He was in total character, his old self, as he entered the hospital. He followed the signs to the intensive care unit.

Outside the ICU stood the boy's parents. He recognized them from TV and, well—they had no problem recognizing him.

Why, hello there! he boomed with a big grin.

Hi, said the father, meekly.

I'm excited to be here—shall we...?

Something seemed wrong. It suddenly occurred to him that perhaps there'd been a complication. He hoped and prayed that the boy hadn't fallen back into a coma or worse.

An uncomfortable pause.

We talked it over... said the mother, almost in a whisper, looking to her husband. The husband wrapped a supportive arm around his wife.

What she means is... look, this is hard, buddy. But we really don't want to risk re-traumatizing our son. It was, after all, a clown that triggered him and you...

The father waved his free hand as if fluffing up something.

I am a clown, yes. But I'm not *that* clown anymore. Can't you see?

I, Clown

Yes, we understand, said the mother, but we just can't take a chance that... you know.

I'm sorry, said the father.

The clown tried to remain smiling through all this, but it was too hard. He bowed his head and mumbled: Okay, I understand.

Then he looked up, forced a smile and insisted: No, really—I do.

The husband batted his fist against an oversized button that opened the twin doors to the ICU, eager to be done with this unpleasant interaction. Like the elevators, electronic doors in hospitals take forever to open. During this protracted, awkward wait, he suddenly remembered—

Hold up. Sorry—listen, he said, I brought some goodies for him.

He handed over the bag and the parents peered inside. Mother reached in and pulled out a drawing pad with multi-colored pens. She held it up, confused.

The clown said: I heard on the news that he was artistic.

This seemed to confirm something between the mother and father. The mother nodded and the two parents quickly passed through the twin doors, which seemed to close faster than they opened.

Thanks, said the father, over his shoulder just before the doors shut.

For many minutes, he stood there in the hall, alone, until a uniformed delivery girl rushed by grasping a big bunch of balloons. The delivery girl stopped, turned around and removed a single red balloon from the bunch and gave it to him.

She winked and grinned before going on her way.

Red balloon in hand, the clown smiled.

Robert Morgan Fisher won the 2018 Chester Himes Fiction Prize and was shortlisted for the 2019 John Steinbeck Award. His fiction and essays have appeared in *Pleiades, Teach. Write., The Wild Word, The Arkansas Review, Red Wheelbarrow, The Missouri Review Soundbooth Podcast, Dime Show Review, 0-Dark-Thirty, The Huffington Post, Psychopomp, The Seattle Review, The Spry Literary Journal, 34th Parallel, The Journal of Microliterature, Spindrift, The Rumpus, Bluerailroad* and many other publications. He has a story in the 2016 Skyhorse Books definitive anthology on speculative war fiction, *Deserts of Fire* and in the 2018 Winterwolf Press *Howl of the Wild Anthology.* He's written for TV, radio and film. Robert holds an MFA in Creative Writing from Antioch University Los Angeles and is currently on the teaching faculty of Antioch University Santa Barbara. Since 2016, Robert has led an acclaimed twice-weekly writing workshop for veterans with PTSD in conjunction with UCLA. He often writes companion songs to his short stories. Both his music and fiction have won many awards. Robert also voices audiobooks. (www.robertmorganfisher.com)

Fear the Clown

Ray Kolb

Garland blamed John Wayne Gacy the most. Sick bastard was the scariest-looking clown he'd ever seen. Like everyone else, Garland had seen the photograph of Gacy standing in his clown suit, on the front steps of someone's home. The look in Gacy's eyes, that evil smile, with the expectation and the knowledge that you'll let him in, let him next to your kids, not suspecting what malevolent thoughts are behind that clown smile. If not Gacy, then there was that psychotic clown from that Stephen King story who comes out of the drain of the high school gym showers and then turns into whatever a person's worst fears are. That was one scary ass clown too. But he—Pennywise, that was his name—wasn't real. John Wayne Gacy was a real monster.

For whatever reason, Gacy or Pennywise or maybe a sick fuckin' perverted uncle who dressed up as a clown just so he could get close to his nephew, the kid wouldn't stop screaming. All Garland could do was stand there with his red bulb nose, his pink and blue Afro, his white powdered face, and his big floppy red shoes, and listen to the kid scream.

Fear the Clown

Garland looked from the boy, who was ten years old today, to the kid's father, a big brawny guy with slicked back oily hair and a nice powder blue buttoned up shirt open to expose his wife-beater undershirt. Classy, Garland thought.

The father looked like he was about to rear back and pop the kid with a backhand to shut him up. Garland tensed, knowing that in the end it didn't make much of a difference, but ready to jump in and do something about it nonetheless.

Just then the mother, a surprisingly attractive woman considering the ugly dump of a turd her husband was, came into the room and went straight for her son. She pulled him close to her bosom and Garland was suddenly jealous of the kid. He wondered if he started crying would she do the same for him. For the first time since he'd entered the home, Garland smiled.

The kid kicked up his screaming a notch, pointing at Garland and claiming the clown was grinning scarily at him. Garland swallowed his smile and looked away.

The father ran a big hand through his hair, looked disgustedly at his son, and turned and walked away. Because Garland was standing near the only door to the room, the father walked just past him, muttering to himself about how much of a pussy his son was. Garland tensed again, liking the father less and less by the minute.

Garland waited a few seconds and then turned around so he could leave the room. Without a clown around, Garland hoped the mother could calm the child. He didn't know if he'd still be performing for the birthday boy and the other kids or not. But either way, he needed the father to pay him.

Before Garland had taken two steps, the mother spoke up.

"Please," she said, "don't go."

Garland turned, his painted clown eyes wide open, wondering if she was actually talking to him. She nodded to Garland and waived him over.

"I don't think that's a good idea, Miss," Garland said. "The kid doesn't seem to like hanging around clowns."

"And the best way to get rid of that fear," she said, standing up but keeping a hand on her son's shoulder, "is to see that there is no reason for such a fear."

The boy, upon his mother pulling away if only a little, cried harder and tried to wrap himself around her leg. He buried his face on her side and, once again, Garland envied the boy.

Garland forced himself to make eye contact with the mother. She was definitely pretty. Blond, with a nice figure, probably not much older than thirty. She reminded him a little of his former wife, before she'd left him because of what he did for a living, before he'd had to enter the Witness Protection Program never to have any contact with any family again. The fact that he was no longer married and never had kids had seemed to make Garland a smart choice for the FBI to target him as their rat. There wasn't anything that the Pantano family could do to hurt Garland once he was inside the program.

But Frank Pantano, *capo* for the Mafia's eastern region near Baltimore, had found the way. He ordered the murder of Garland's brother, and had threatened his brother's family, a wife and two kids, a boy and a girl, to keep Garland quiet. It had worked. Not that Garland had been particularly close to his brother, his sister-in-law, or his niece and nephew. But they were the only living family he had.

Garland refused to testify and left the program despite the threats of the FBI to put him in a hole until he was ninety. Garland went into hiding, from both the feds and the Pantanos. But he had a plan.

He'd always had a plan. It had taken four years to come to fruition but his plan was now happening.

Frank Pantano had killed his brother, so Garland would do the same. He'd decided to kill the whole family, to let Pantano know he could hit back even harder if Pantano wanted to keep playing this game. Of course, if everything went right, Pantano would never know who actually killed his brother. Only that it was revenge for something. Garland would make sure Pantano knew that.

Garland didn't relish the idea of having to kill the wife and kid. They seemed so normal, so likable. Not that he hadn't done such things in the past, in his old life, but never like this, up this close and personal.

Killing Frank Pantano's brother, Louis, would be a pleasure. As soon as Garland was alone with the bastard, he'd cut his throat and stab him in his chest and stomach a few times, a clear sign to Frank Pantano that this was a revenge killing. Garland would let Louis die at his feet and then get the hell away. No one would be able to identify him. The clown makeup was a perfect disguise. He would kill the mother and kid quickly with two bullets each between the eyes. No need for either to suffer. It was the least he could do for them.

"If you could take the wig and nose off, maybe that would help."

Garland snapped out of his reverie. The mother was smiling at him, hoping he'd help her calm the kid, who was still crying and hiding his face.

The last thing Garland wanted to do was remove part of his disguise. He'd have to kill everyone at the party otherwise. He didn't know if even he could get away with killing forty people at one time. No doubt some of Louis Pantano's friends would be armed.

"Tell you what," Garland said. He squatted down, making himself eye level with the kid. He took off his nose but left the Afro wig on. "How about if young Mr. Pantano here puts on the nose. I promise you, you can't be upset when you're wearing a clown nose." Garland squeezed the nose, which honked like a stork that had been goosed. He noticed the smile from Mrs. Pantano.

The kid stopped crying for half a second and glanced to see where the noise came from. He saw the nose in Garland's hand, almost smiled, and then looked back at Garland and started crying again. Although not with as much intensity as before. Garland felt the tiniest bit of satisfaction.

Mrs. Pantano bent down to soothe her kid and spoke to him in a calming voice. "Paul," she said. "Go ahead and put the nose on. It'll be fun."

Paul Pantano shook his head but his crying lessened a little more. He shot a quick glance toward Garland and stuck his head back on his mother's leg again.

"Tell you what I'm going to do, Paul," Garland said, looking over his shoulder in an over-the-top conspiratorial fashion and then back to the kid. "Something that I've never done before. And it's something that is actually against the Clown Laws set up by the Clown Government, which is somewhere over in Europe." Garland enjoyed the growing smile from Mrs. Pantano.

The kid was still crying but was now paying attention. Garland removed his oversized red shoes. "Because I can tell that deep down you actually really like clowns, I'm going to let you wear my clown shoes."

Paul Pantano stopped crying completely and stood with his mouth wide open. He looked at his mother and then back to Garland. "Can I really?"

Garland was about to answer when he heard Louis Pantano yell from another room, "Maria, get your ass in here now! I can't find the fuckin' party hats!"

Maria Pantano looked at Garland briefly, with an embarrassed sad smile, and then turned to her son. "I'll be right back, okay? I've got to help your father. Can you stay here with…" She turned to Garland for help.

Garland stammered for a moment, captivated by how radiant Maria Pantano had looked with her cheeks flushed red and her eyes looking at him for compassion and understanding. It took him a few beats to remember the clown name he'd come up with and been booked under for this gig. As he remembered, he really wished he'd come up with something better.

"Uh … it's Happy the Clown." Now it was Garland's turn to blush. He was glad he had the white makeup on.

"Okay, Happy the Clown it is," Maria Pantano said. She turned back to her son. "Can you stay with Happy for a minute?"

Paul Pantano seemed to seriously contemplate the choice, looking from his mother to Garland to the clown shoes in rapid succession. Finally, he nodded and reached for the shoes.

Maria Pantano sighed, stood up, placing a hand on Garland's forearm just above his oversized white clown gloves, and mouthed, "Thank you." Then she hurriedly left the room as her husband started yelling again.

Garland enjoyed the residual tingling on his arm where Maria Pantano had touched him and didn't catch what the kid said at first. Garland forced himself out of his daydreaming about the kid's mother and focused on the words.

Garland sat down and motioned for Paul Pantano to do the same. The kid complied, crossing his legs just as Garland had done. When Garland reached up to scratch the itch around his nose where the glue had held his clown nose in place, the kid scratched his nose in the same way. Garland smiled. It reminded him of how his nephew would imitate his brother during the few times he'd managed to visit with them.

"We need to be careful," Garland said. "I've already given you a lot of clown power with the nose and the shoes. According to Clown Law, someone training to be a clown can only handle so much at one time, and only then after years of special clown training."

Paul Pantano crinkled his forehead and looked down and Garland was worried he'd start crying again. Instead, the kid raised his head, his eyes serious, and nodded. "I understand. And I accept the responsibility."

Garland smiled widely. "Good boy." Without thinking, he reached over and tussled Paul Pantano's hair. The kid tensed and started to pull back but didn't. Garland wondered what bad things in the past had triggered that instinctive response from the boy.

Over the next ten minutes, Garland helped Paul Pantano act like a clown. He put the clown nose over the boy's nose. Both of them squeezed it several times, laughing together as it let out its annoying honking noise. Garland put the clown shoes over the kid's own shoes and laughed as he tried to walk around in them, falling over several times. Garland hadn't enjoyed himself this much since... since a long time. After the necessary business of today was over, he was going to check on his brother's family, to see how they were doing. He knew he probably couldn't contact them for fear of putting them in danger again. But he at least wanted to know.

"Do you think I could wear your clown hair too?"

There was no way Garland was going to give the kid his Afro wig. He'd already given everyone too much of a look of his face by handing over the nose. But he didn't want to hurt the kid's feelings or, even worse, set him off on another crazy banshee-wailing binge. But no wig meant no more kid.

It was at that moment that Garland realized he wasn't going to whack the kid or his mother. He felt good about that. Killing the father would be good enough.

Maria Pantano came back into the room, watched the two of them together for a few moments, and then told them that it was time to start the party. Paul Pantano grabbed Garland's hand and led the way to the backyard.

Overall the party went well. The children played games, the mothers watched their children have fun. The handful of fathers who were there hung out together near the back of the yard, enjoying the alcohol and food. Garland had performed his ten-minute routine, told a few lame jokes, twisted a couple of balloon animals, snuck a couple of quick looks down the tops of some of the mothers' low cut dresses and tops, including Maria Pantano's. For the most part, Louis Pantano behaved himself, spending most of his time talking a little too loud among the group at the rear of the party. Only once had he shouted his disapproval at his wife for something that was subpar about the party.

After a couple of hours, the party wound down and most of the guests went home. Paul's best friend, Peter, and Peter's mother and father, who seemed to be the best friends of the adult Pantanos, stayed late. Paul and Peter were excited to spend more time together and were also worn out from the party. Their mothers encouraged the boys to take a nap so they could be ready for dinner later. They verbally fought the idea but easily let themselves be led to Paul's bedroom upstairs. Garland was glad the kid would be far away when he whacked his dad.

As expected, Louis Pantano was to pay Garland his fee at the end of the party. Pantano, even though Garland estimated the man had consumed at least a dozen drinks, didn't seem fazed by the alcohol intake at all. Pantano led Garland into his office, on the ground floor in the rear of the house. What Garland hadn't planned on was that the other kid's father would tag along. It would be a little tougher, killing them both, particularly since both men were taller and larger than Garland, but it wasn't a situation that Garland hadn't successfully faced before.

Garland calmly brought along his small black bag that looked like a nineteenth-century doctor's bag. He'd used it in his birthday party routine, pulling out balloons and the water pistol he'd used to squirt the kids. As soon as the three of them were alone, Garland pulled out his gun, with silencer attached, and shot Pantano's friend twice in the chest and then once in the forehead. The corpse dropped to the carpet of the room before Pantano knew his friend was dead.

"What the fuck?" Pantano started backing away, reaching behind him for his desk and, Garland had no doubt, a hidden gun somewhere nearby.

Garland hit him hard on his forehead with the gun. Without raising his voice, he said, "Stop moving, asshole."

Pantano stopped. "What do you want?" He rubbed the spot on his forehead that was quickly rising and turning red.

"I want you to send a message to your brother," Garland said.

"Frank?"

"No," Garland said, "Your other brother, Mickey Mouse." Garland hit him with his gun on the forehead again. "Of course, I mean Frank." Garland noticed, almost in passing, how easily he had slipped back into his old personality. Since just before shooting Pantano's friend, Garland had been cool, emotionless. A hardened professional calmly performing his trade. His trade had been murder. And he'd been good at it.

"Please," Pantano said, "I'll tell Frank whatever you want. Just stop hitting me in the fucking head."

Garland nodded. He used the gun as a pointer and said, "Now turn around and get on your knees."

"Oh God, no," Pantano said, his voice rising, the fear palpable. "Please don't shoot me. I've got a family. A son."

"I'm not going to shoot you," Garland said. "As long as you do as I say and turn around and get on your knees."

Pantano nodded but clearly didn't believe him. Even so, he turned his back to Garland and then dropped to his knees. Garland hadn't lied to him. He wasn't going to shoot Pantano. Garland put his gun back into the black bag and pulled out a ten-inch hunting knife with a serrated edge. He grabbed Pantano by the hair, put the knife to the man's throat and quickly sliced through his Adam's apple and carotid artery. Garland held Pantano's head up so he could bleed more quickly, stabbed him a couple of times in the chest and once in the gut, and then wiped the blade on the back of Pantano's shirt and then pushed him away in disgust.

Garland listened to Pantano gurgle and choke, and watched as the body twitched slower and slower. Satisfied that Pantano was dead or very soon would be, Garland turned to put the knife back into his bag and then get out of the house as soon as possible.

Standing in the doorway, his mouth and eyes as wide as could be, was Paul Pantano.

Garland had driven two hundred miles on the interstate before he finally couldn't take it anymore. It was getting close to midnight and he pulled off on a lonely exit with just a couple of working streetlights and found a dive bar with only a handful of patrons. He pounded one shot of whiskey after another until the bartender politely suggested he slow it down a bit. Garland told the bartender to fuck off and mind his own business and to pour him another drink. When the bartender brought the bottle for another pour, Garland grabbed the bottle and moved to a table against the wall. The bartender smartly refrained from commenting.

Garland took a big swig of the whiskey and closed his eyes. He couldn't get the look on Paul Pantano's face out of his mind. And he couldn't get the scream of terror deep from within the kid's bones out of his ears.

Garland should have shot the kid, as soon as he started screaming. He would have done so before. And then, once you kill the kid, the kid's mother, friend, and the friend's mother would have to be next. Instead, Garland had run away as fast as he could, through the only way out available, the door where Paul Pantano was standing. The kid's eyes looked as if they were going to pop out, watching the murderous clown coming straight at him. The kid had run away, screaming at the top of his lungs, heading for God knows what hiding place, hoping the clown who'd murdered his father wouldn't find him. Whatever fears Paul Pantano had had of clowns before this day were nothing compared to the nightmares he was going to have from now on.

Gacy and Pennywise had nothing on Happy the Clown.

Garland slammed another shot of whiskey. He didn't think he'd be paying a visit to his brother's widow and their children after all.

Fear the Clown

Ray Kolb's stories have appeared in a number of venues, including *Refractions*, *Hides the Dark Tower*, and *Manor House*.

Replevin

Misha Burnett

He was wrong and I was right.

That doesn't make me feel any better about myself, but it is a fact, something to keep in mind.

The car was a Chrysler LeBaron, 2 door coupe, red in color. Five year loan, signed seventeen months ago. Delinquent on payments, three months, sent to legal, judge signed the writ of replevin, and the file came to me.

I worked for American Auto Recovery, which was owned by Bluebird Finance, which also owned a half dozen used car lots that changed names so often that the salesmen got paid with counter checks, to save on printing costs.

Welcome to the looking glass world of used car sales.

It was five in the morning and the sun was painting the sky over the desert in the colors of an infected wound.

I'd looked through the file in the cab. The debtor had been working in the warehouse of department store when he signed the loan. He'd quit that job, which was when he stopped making payments. He'd also changed his phone number, and the registered letters we'd sent hadn't been signed for.

Replevin

It's funny, but most people on the run don't run far. I'd located the car within a few miles of his last address.

The cab took me past the apartment building lot and I saw the flash of red in the early morning light. It was still there, so I paid the cab and got out.

The key codes were in the file, of course, that's standing operating procedure when you advertise that you'll finance anybody.

So I had the keys in my hand, walking slowly up to the car, not running, not sneaking around, just walking normally like I had every right to be there.

Took a good look at the back seat as I walked up. Full of junk, brightly colored clothes strewn around, a couple of suitcases, some toys, balls and costume hats, like some ogre ate a circus and puked it up into the car's back seat. No human sized lumps, though, not quite enough junk that a person could be under all that crap. I made sure of that as I ambled up.

Then I was at the door and, yes, the key worked the door, and I slid inside and the key worked the ignition, too. Pulled out of the space, looking in all directions at once, but nobody else was anywhere around. Still asleep. Probably nobody saw me pull out of the lot.

Even though it had become a job and just as boring and routine as any other way of paying the bills, I always had one moment of adrenaline. From unlocking the car door to getting out of view of the pick up site—maybe two minutes of cold sweat, every time.

Then I was on the main drag and past the fear window, figuring my route back to the yard.

Being in a stranger's car is a curious feeling. In some ways it's more intimate than being in a stranger's home. Homes are deliberate places.

Cars, though, they hold the traces of the things you do while you're driving, which are almost always things that you don't really think about.

Being in a stranger's car can feel like climbing in through a stranger's bedroom window.

There were business cards scattered across the passenger seat. At a stop light I picked one up and looked at it.

ALEX THE HAPPY CLOWN, it said. Parties, Fundraisers, Company Picnics, Family Reunions. With a phone number and some clip art of a bunch of balloons.

A couple of weeks ago I had taken my daughter to a church carnival. Not my church, I didn't have a church. But one of the other little girls in the neighborhood had invited my daughter, so I took her. A few dollars donation and a fun afternoon, the usual attractions. A few rides, anemic enough to amuse fourth graders without terrifying their parents, a pen full of goats wide-eyed in fearless wonder at being fed by giggling children, some ponies.

Clowns.

My daughter sat perfectly still to have a butterfly painted on her cheek and didn't wash her face for a week, until the paint had flaked off to the point where you couldn't tell what the design was supposed to be. She took home a balloon dinosaur and insisted on taking it to bed with her. I knew it wouldn't last the night and it didn't and when she saw it in rags in the morning she cried.

Alex the Happy Clown would get his stuff back, the crazy colored clothes and the suitcase of magic tricks. So long as he could find someone to give him a ride to the office and had some ID, he could pick up any personal items left in the car.

They probably wouldn't do him a lot of good without a car, though. Without a car he'd probably have to go back to working in a warehouse.

I parked the Chrysler in the lot behind the chain link and razor wire and went to the office. I handed over the file and the keys to the car, and then I handed over the rest of my keys. I didn't think about it, I didn't know I was going to do it until I saw my ring on his desk.

"I can't do this any more," I said.

My boss didn't argue with me, didn't try to keep me on. He just took the keys and told me to let the secretary at the finance company know I was quitting. He didn't ask me why.

I had to wonder if he figured it out when he saw the last car I'd brought in.

I went back home to my daughter. I got another job right away, working at a convenience store on the graveyard shift. A man who wants to work can always find a job doing something.

––––––––

Misha Burnett has little formal education, but has been writing poetry and fiction for around forty years. During this time he has supported himself and his family with a variety of jobs, including locksmith, cab driver, and building maintenance.

His first four novels, *Catskinner's Book*, *Cannibal Hearts*, *The Worms Of Heaven*, and *Gingerbread Wolves* comprise a series, collectively known as *The Book Of Lost Doors*.

Major influences include Tim Powers, Samuel Delany, William Burroughs, and Phillip K. Dick.

More information about upcoming projects can be found at http://mishaburnett.wordpress.com

Corn Stalker

Dan Allen

Long after the brightest days were gone, and the sky turned perpetually grey, darkness came early, and harvest season ended. An eager frost burned what wasn't already brown and strong northern winds threatened rain or worse. As if in denial of the encroaching gloom, children and adults, intoxicated by festivity, desired to be frightened.

On a night peppered with a contradiction of sounds, blood-chilling screams mixed with joyful laughter, a man slipped between rows of dried-out cornstalks and joined others already hidden in the maze. Crouching low, he watched and waited, dressed the same as the actors, each decorated in the scariest of costumes and painted with theatrical makeup. They were supposed to be there, paid to terrify the ticket-buying public, he wasn't. The ground felt hard as cement having given up the last of the summer heat and it offered no comfort. A chill spiked the air and his breath floated around him like low-lying fog. He imagined it boiling from his mouth and spreading over the field to further obscure his fun.

Leaves crunched, and he heard giggling as they approached. They passed within inches of his feet but failed to see him, too busy being silly and pushing against each other. They dared to take a peek into the shadows and flinched at nothing.

He could have snuck up behind them and perhaps walk along for a few steps before he pulled his trick, but no. This group wasn't what he wanted. He would wait for someone special. A minute later from further in the maze, squeals and laughter broke the silence.

Despite numb fingertips under his thin white gloves, his face became uncomfortably warm and his cheeks stuck to the mask. He wanted to take it off, but it offered anonymity and fueled his thrill. The evil clown costume was brilliant, and he wondered why he hadn't thought of it before. The ridiculously over-sized meat cleaver added to the terror and his only regret not bringing along a balloon.

He loved the mask, despite its weird smell and the face sweats it causes. It made him feel strong and invincible. Behind this disguise, he could act out his fantasies and kill whoever he wanted. Others wore masks but his was the best with its exaggerated smile and grotesque pointed teeth.

A breeze whistled through the stalks and the temperature dropped another few degrees. An orange glow crept over the southern horizon and he smiled. The fall was his most-loved time of the year and Halloween his favorite celebration. A festival of dress up, make-believe, and death. More screams shattered the crystal air, followed by schoolgirl laughter. He wished they would take this more seriously. He wanted his kill to be perfect and it would spoil his fun if they weren't afraid. He would make them, when he got his chance, but for now he had to wait his turn and hope he didn't miss all the fun.

Dark and winding, the path ventured far from the crowds and deep into the field. Littered with monsters ready to jump and scare the bejesus out of you, the maze provided an unnerving walk, perfect for getting into the spirit of the season. The actors weren't allowed to touch the guests. For him, this wasn't enough. He snuck in through the back woods and made his own rules.

A twig cracked, and he adjusted his mask. Someone else walked the maze.

"I'm cold, Daddy."

"Ok, honey. We're almost to the end."

This one wasn't right. He wouldn't do children. Their little lives were all ready messed up. His arms tightened, urges and desires became poison in his veins. He needed release and he prayed it would come soon.

The enormous harvest moon cleared the horizon and looked like a giant pumpkin. Far down the row, stalks bent and swayed back into place. Something approached, and it rolled in on him like a rogue wave. A zombie burst from darkness and plopped himself down.

"Hey, bro. How the scares been going? Man, I got some kids earlier, I swear they shit their pants," said the talking corpse.

"Go away," replied the man.

"Chill, dude. We can tag team the next group. This is what we signed up for, my brother."

"I work alone, now piss off." The clown stood and towered over the zombie. His eyes glowed orange, reflecting the moon and he growled.

"Relax, dude. I'm going. Have fun, man. I'll catcha later."

A flash of yellow caught his eye, perhaps a rain coat, and once again he made ready. A gust of wind sent a stream of leaves twisting and turning. Behind him, corn shafts rustled and he heard the far away cry of an owl.

For a moment, disappointment dampened his excitement and he feared no more would come.

He heard voices. Young boys, rowdy and disrespectful, crashed through the maze, deliberately destroying parts of the path.

"I see you, Mr. Clown," said one dressed in an old Jean-jacket, probably stolen out of the back of his father's closet.

"Ya, ugly face. You don't scare us," added another. He puffed on a cigarette and held it between his finger tips as if he planned to throw it at a dartboard.

The third stayed quiet. Obviously the smartest of the trio.

The clown growled and backed into the shadows. He bit his lip to control his rage and let them pass, never having had the opportunity to take them by surprise.

Something delicious approached. She smelled like baked apples and cinnamon. He inhaled her essence and held it as long as he could. She wore a long coat and left it unbuttoned so it flowed behind her like a cape. Pink shorts left too much exposed for such a cold night and he crawled closer to see her milky white legs. No pantyhose, bare and flawless, her legs raced to the sky and met her cascading hair halfway. Somewhere in the back of his head, the halleluiah choir sang, and he imagined a moonbeam flowed over her, lighting her way with an orange spotlight. He tingled, his senses as crisp as the air.

He shifted up on his haunches and held the twelve-inch meat cleaver with a firm grip. More leaves crunched, and he heard a second set of footsteps, heavier and loud. A boyfriend perhaps, but it didn't matter, he needed to do this and couldn't wait any longer. His plan was simple, let them pass and chop them on the back of the neck. He would disappear into corn rows and run away. He wouldn't get caught. He didn't even work there. No one saw him come in and no one would see him leave. If it all went as planned, he might even come back next year and do it again.

He was surprised how quiet it was in the late fall. No cicadas sang or crickets chirpped, even the birds seemed to have disappeared. Later at night, the coyotes would howl, but there was only silence and he heard his knees crack when he stood. The lovers, for that's what they were, held hands and whispered and failed to hear. He raised the cleaver above his head and with both hands brought it down on the back of the boyfriend's neck. He aimed for the sweet spot, above the collar and below the hairline. The man went down like someone opened a trap door beneath his feet.

The girl turned to face him, and her hand emerged from her purse. He heard a little pop and caught a flash of silver reflected by the moonlight. The stiletto switchblade punctured his skin and sunk into his side. Her arm quivered and she pushed the knife up and held it in for an extra second. He peered through the holes in his mask and made eye contact. He saw fear in her face and watched her eyes well up. Her mouth hung open, but no sound came out, and tears began to flow. Her jaw trembled, and her pupils grew large. She pulled the stiletto out and plunged it into his chest. The thin blade slid nicely between his ribs and found its mark. She released the knife and backed away. Her adrenalin spent, she shivered and dropped to her knees. His meat cleaver, a large plastic clown prop covered with purple polka dots, hit the ground and he followed.

"Jesus, honey. It was just a toy," said the boyfriend as he rubbed the welt on his neck.

"I didn't know. I thought he was for real, I mean, I thought he cut you," she said. "My god, did I kill him?"

"He might not be dead. Leave him and we'll go get help."

He heard their muffled words and rested his face against the frozen ground. Beneath him, a crimson puddle expanded a stain that wouldn't be seen until daylight. Soon, all alone, he looked for the moon, but only found blackness. He needed to get better at fulfilling his murder fantasy, and he still liked his plan, a real monster hiding amongst the pretend. He thought next time he would try the Haunted House. Seconds later, he thought nothing at all.

Dan Allen is Canadian and enjoys spending time off the grid in Northern Ontario. His story "Above the Ceiling" (Originally published in *Home Sweet Home* by Millhaven Press, September 2018) is featured in Bards and Sages annual anthology of *The Year's Best Speculative Fiction*.

Most recently Alban Lake Publishing has acquired his story "Sympathy for the Zingara" for the March 2019 return of *ParABnormal Magazine*. His work also appears in 2018's Top Science Fiction/Horror anthology - Secret Stairs: A Tribute to Urban Legend. (#1 Best Seller - Amazon)

Other recent releases include *Bringing It Back* from Horrified Press, May 2018, *Canadian Creatures* from Schreyer Ink, June 2018, *Through the Dark Vol 2* from Celenic Earth, August 2018, *Haunted Holidays* from Thirteen O'clock Press, October 2018, and *CultureCult Magazine*, January 2019.

Dan recently survived ninety minutes with Mr. Deadman on the Deadman's Tome Podcast. You'll find it online.

You can visit Dan at www.danallenhorror.com and follow him on Facebook and Twitter at @danallenhorror. You can write to Dan at contact@danallenhorror.com

The Distinguished Gentleman

M. Kelly Peach

Reggie walks the runway between the bleachers. They are packed with circus fans. He sees the Ringmaster, spotlighted and starting his introductory spiel. As Reggie nears the center ring, the pungent smells of the big top fill his nostrils: an intermingling of fresh popcorn, caramel apples, grease paint, the body scents of thousands of spectators, animal dung, and cotton candy. His adrenalin is flowing. His stride quickens, becomes more confident. This is what he loves to do—what he lives for.

"...Ladies and gentlemen, I present, for his final performance, the world-renowned Reginald, The Distinguished Gentleman!" cries the Ringmaster in his booming voice.

Reggie slips into performance mode for the last time. To his surprise, he finds he is as nervous as he was for his first performance six decades ago. The transformation into a distinguished gentleman begins, but not just any gentleman. He is indeed a world-famous circus gentleman—a headliner—his features as well-known as A-list movie actors or super star athletes. Nobody can do the classic Breakfast Scene with his trademark flourish and snap opening of the morning paper like Reggie.

To the accustomed cheers and applause—the very life blood of his existence for so many years, less enthusiastic now with the crowd comprised of the younger generation and their children—the star of the show steps into the spotlight.

The open-walled scene with kitchen and adjoining study is waiting for him in the middle of the center ring and all the props are set up exactly where he has demanded.

He strides to the kitchen area and goes into his Breakfast before Work Routine—second only, in fame and popularity, to his Coming Home from the Office Routine. Like most circus gentlemen, he never utters a word in his act. His movements have an exaggerated, yet controlled, expressiveness to convey his comedic intention. Many in the crowd are familiar with his act and howl with mirth, much of it anticipatory, at each part of his performance.

He starts by making the coffee and toast. While the bread is turning to a perfect golden brown and the java is brewing, he retrieves the folded morning newspaper by opening the stand-alone front door near, but separate from, the study, walking through it, and stooping down to pick it up from the ground. He gently wipes the few bits of sawdust clinging to the paper as he retreats back through the doorframe and carefully closes the door.

He places the newspaper on the breakfast nook table in the corner of the kitchen as, with impeccable timing, the bell for the toaster rings, the crisped bread pops up, and the coffee-maker beeps to indicate the coffee is ready. He moves to the toaster and plucks at the hot pieces of bread pretending to burn his finger-tips. The audience laughs as he tries again, with greater care, and manages to transfer them to the Wedgwood Queen's Ware white, gold-trimmed bone china bread plate—the only suitable dinnerware for a gentleman—next to the toaster.

They are buttered with a genuine silver plate, twisted handle, Savoy pattern butter knife—the only suitable silverware for a gentleman—from Roger Brothers. More audience members chuckle at how fastidiously he covers every square centimeter of each piece. None of them notices the dab of butter he drops on the table because it is hidden behind the plate's golden rim. This has never happened before in his long career; he is famous for the flawlessness of his routines.

The gaff causes the briefest of hesitations, imperceptible to the spectators. He finishes the buttering, moves the plate to the breakfast nook, then goes to the coffee-maker.

The glass pot is taken from under the spout and he fills a delicate cup resting on a saucer. Both match the Wedgwood china plate. The coffee, made from an outrageously expensive premium blend of Jamaican beans and *Supremo Arabica* Colombian. It is very dark and rich... the only coffee good enough for a truly distinguished gentleman...not a drop is spilled. He disdains cream and sugar, will only drink it black.

The cup and saucer are carried in both hands to the breakfast area. Half way there, his hands begin trembling and start the dishes rattling. A small amount, less than a teaspoon, of spillage is incurred. He is dismayed but manages to hide it from the audience. They laugh, are delighted thinking it is a new refinement in this, his final act.

With a tinkling of a tiny silver bell, which sounds to his ears like a blacksmith's hammer striking an anvil, he sets cup and saucer next to the plate with toast and takes a seat on the blonde pine wood breakfast nook bench. Wincing internally at the unplanned waste of precious restorative, he ad-libs and takes a paper napkin from the holder in the center of the table and mops the saucer and bottom of his gold-trimmed china cup, tosses the napkin off to the side. After a sip of coffee, he smartly, yet carefully, opens the tattered Wall Street Journal—his favorite prop.

A stickler for details, he feels a real gentleman would read only The Journal so he had gone to great trouble and expense, at the beginning of his career, to obtain an old, genuine edition of the paper. It has become yellowed, frangible, and, despite his unfailing solicitude, battered from its years of use in the show.

In leisurely fashion, he alternates between nibbles of the first piece of toast and measured sips of coffee while perusing the same article for every performance. The first slice is finished when the cup is exactly half-empty. In his world, it is never half-full. The second piece is taken up and he continues reading and supping. The crowd chortles with every bite and tipple. Their mirth increases when he has to turn several pages to where the column has been continued.

The article, given his precise rate of ingestion, is, to the second, the correct length in terms of timing. Though other circus gentleman might fake it, he is a professional and reads it through every time even though he has done it so often he knows the words by heart.

Reginald finishes the article, first cup of coffee, and toast at precisely the same time. His act is nearly over.

He folds the paper and puts it under his left arm, arises from the bench, pours himself another cup, and walks over to the open study area with its easy-chair. It is a genuine Laz-y-Boy with real leather upholstery. On one side is a brass floor lamp with Tiffany-style butterfly shade and on the other is an Ethan Allen cherry wood Georgian Court end table. The three furnishings are vintage, mid-twentieth century.

Halfway there he goes into his trademark gesture of a stylized stumble. It is a simple, classic yet elegant homage to his, and the audience's, heroes and forefathers. The spillage, planned this time, of one and a half tablespoons of the coffee into the saucer is accomplished with the usual exacting flair. He removes the dainty cup from saucer, and with little finger lifted high, brings the small plate to lips and slurps the dark brown liquid.

The crowd laughs uproariously and he takes a second to look over the saucer at a child in the front row—one he had surreptitiously pre-selected, as he always does, early in the act as he was making toast. The saucer is lowered and cup placed back into it as Reginald, breaking character, winks and grins mischievously at the child. They love it and laugh even harder.

The audience is larger than he thought. The stands are completely filled; mostly with families as is to be expected. There are a lot of traditional faces but also a nice mix of original facial stylings. As usual, there are a few devoted fans emulating his basic style and dress with just a few minor alterations to give themselves some all-important uniqueness.

In the brief moment he looks into the stands, he also notices the typical mayhem one would find with any large assembly. There's a Pennywise trying to coax a little Milky the Clown to come sit by him.

He thinks, "I wouldn't do that, young fellow."

A nearby Emmet Kelly type is squirting the plastic flower in his lapel at an *auguste* sitting in front of him. Close by is a Bozo-like adolescent bopping his Lou Jacob friend over the head with an oversized foam rubber hammer. Two rows lower is a near-Coco and two of his friends in the middle of their Busy Bee routine spraying an Adleresque whiteface teenager with water. Next to them is a Rebo look-alike folding balloons for a dozen raggedy rodeo clown tykes seated around him.

It is difficult to tell what the crowd's laughter is about: Reginald's performance or the antics of its own members. No matter, he is a consummate professional inured to these distractions. He strolls over to the study and, after placing the cup and saucer on the table, settles into the cool comfort of the easy-chair to finish his newspaper and coffee. The small, contained riot in the stands continues as he takes his time and finishes the coffee and newspaper, simultaneously and with aplomb and dignity.

As the spotlights slowly fade, the audience realizes the act has come to its close and ceases its shenanigans. Fueled by the knowledge this is his final performance, they leap to their feet screaming their delight, honking their rubber-bulb horns, stomping in their over-sized shoes, and clapping deliriously so that the applause, the last he will ever hear, is thunderous.

As soon as he exits the main ring, the spotlights come up and the Ringmaster enters, strikes a pose with black top hat lifted high. Already striding down the passageway between the bleachers, he can hear from behind him deep, theatrical bellowing, "The one, the only, Reginald! The greatest distinguished gentleman of them all!"

The crowd erupts into even louder cheering as he makes his way to the decrepit twenty-three-foot trailer, an ancient, modified Airstream Flying Cloud, that has been his office, changing room, and domicile for several decades. By the time he climbs on to the heavy wooden crate he uses as a stool (the trailer's foot step has been gone for years) and opens the trailer door, the audience is listening to the introduction for the next act. The distinguished gentleman who was, outside of the spotlights, anything but a gentleman, knows most of them, in their excitement to see the trapeze artists, will have already forgotten him.

He enters and begins removing his costume. First off are the highly polished, size ten, black, genuine leather wingtips. Very hard to find and expensive, they are, to be perfectly frank, hideous. He sets them next to his comfortable, every day, red plastic size 25 shoes with the flapping toes. Next to go are the black merino wool-nylon blend dress socks... pricey but worth every penny. They are smelly and the left one has a gaping hole at the big toe. He tosses them into the basket for laundering.

The tailored, charcoal gray, three-piece, pin-striped wool suit with a lightly starched, white oxford shirt (stained the color of yellow bile, if one looks closely, around the collar and cuffs) and a crimson silk power tie are deftly shucked and hung on their usual hooks along the wall. He realizes, with a grateful sigh, he will never have to don the suit and loafers again.

Wearing only a sleeveless undershirt and briefs, both of them soiled and ripped in several places, he takes a seat at his small, battered vanity set with splattered make-up mirror. Three, no...it's four now, light bulbs have burned out and the rest are dusty and draped with cobwebs.

He thinks, "Gonna have to get those replaced and the rest wiped down and the old mirror...early twentieth century, picked it up in an antique shop in...was it, Boise? Anyways, get it cleaned up tomorrow...definitely." Except, what would be the point? He won't be putting on his make-up anymore. Reggie takes a deep, shuddering breath and the frightening void in his stomach becomes emptier. He quickly reverses his line of thought, backing away, as he has for the last six months since announcing his retirement, from contemplation of what he will do with his remaining years.

To begin his transformation, he takes off his bald-head wig. It's the one with a fringe of sparse gray hair around the ears and to the back of the head. Knowing it is the little details that separate good performers from great performers, he has combed a few strands over the pate like old geezers would do in the Twentieth Century. What were they thinking? If they had fourteen hairs sideways over their shiny heads nobody would notice they were bald? Did they not realize it in fact only served to emphasize their baldness?

Shaking his head in wonderment at the vagaries of those old-time old-timers, he hangs the wig on the hook attached to the right side of the mirror. As is his habit once the wig is removed, the now ex-circus performer rubs his scalp, bare as any of the burned-out bulbs, with both hands.

He pulls his make-up kit from the drawer, finds the make-up remover towelettes with micellar water, aloe vera, and white tea extracts. Three wipes suffice to eliminate nearly all of the first layer of cover up, second layer of foundation, areas of additional darker, cream-based foundation for contouring, setting powder, subtle blush, and flesh-colored lipstick.

Reggie goes to the tiny kitchen sink, flicks on the water pump, turns the faucet handle, and deep cleans his gaunt face and neck with water and facial cleanser to remove any remaining make-up from his pores. After wiping dry his hands, neck, and face, he returns to the vanity table and recalls a time early in his career when he had to use a black pencil eyeliner to draw lines on his features to create the illusion of wrinkles. His naturally aged face—one could as well say beech wood aged or aged in charred white oak barrels—with a line for every bottle downed, has had more wrinkles than required for his role as a distinguished gentleman for a long time.

He pauses to hunch closer and peer intently into the mirror. An old, washed-up performer's face looks back at him. The whites of his eyes are bloodshot from lack of sleep and jaundiced from too much rye, and the colors in his face are beginning to fade. The baggage under his eyes—a duffel astride a portmanteau—is swollen and discolored with a grayish tint visible through the yellow triangles imprinted above and below both eyes, the broad upturned, happy-mouth in the same yellow, and red circles on the cheekbones. As well-known to circus aficionados as his gentleman's face, Reggie's whiteface, with its facial stylings designed so many years ago with the help of his skin dyist, needs more than some touch-ups.

"When was the last time," the retired distinguished gentleman asks his reflection, "you visited the dyist?"

It has been so long he can't remember and the man in the mirror, the one he steadfastly refuses to make eye-contact with, has no answers. He never does.

Shrugging, he makes a mental note—which will probably be forgotten within minutes—to give a call to Rudolpho. A skin dyist to the stars, he should never be confused with a tattoo artist whom the masses, unwashed and eaters of pork rinds, would use.

Speaking of unwashed, he tries to remember his last shower, thinks it may have been yesterday and lifts his arm to sniff his pit. The sharp sourness, with a bite like a Gila monster, indicates it was more likely the day before yesterday...but could well have been three days ago.

He shrugs and pulls on his favorite daily-wear: a blaring red, green and yellow plaid suit coat (five sizes too big and with the standard issue squirting plastic flower in the lapel) and best patched baggy black trousers (again, five sizes too big) with fluorescent green suspenders.

The make-up kit is searched until the spirit gum is found. The old, red Howle nose is sitting in the right corner of the vanity top, its usual spot, waiting patiently. He picks it up and applies a liberal layer of the adhesive all around the edges and lets it air dry for moment until tacky. In one deft motion, the round acrylic-coated latex appendage is attached with perfect placement over his own snoot and held there for a minute until the spirit gum dries completely.

The last piece of his ensemble, the trademark blaze orange, Phyllis Diller-style fright wig, is plucked from its hook on the left side of the mirror and placed on his head. With a couple of quick tugs, it is expertly and securely fitted.

He swivels around on the vanity bench to slip on his large floppy shoes, their color matching his nose, and then turns back for one last look in the mirror. He makes an unnecessary, miniscule adjustment to his wig and another to the purple lapel flower then looks, finally, into the depths of the mirror...and his own eyes.

If these are the windows to his soul, then his dark brown irises are the color of the hooded curtains he has kept closed over them for these many years. Since puberty, in fact, when his first crush laughed soul-crushingly in his face at a high school dance after his friends divulged to her the secret of his infatuation. As if she would ever go out with such a loser. He didn't even have a car and let's not mention his bubbling acne.

He had both desired and dreaded (for good reason it turned out) to tell her, so his pals had taken it upon themselves to let her know. Since then, if he ever had the notion to perhaps attempt another relationship, the image of her and her two friends pointing at him standing against the gym wall and giggling cruelly as they walked away was replayed in his brain as a reminder to never again be so foolish as to risk opening his heart.

The curtains in his eyes cracked open and all he could see behind them was the fear of his remaining solitary years. He was an only child and both parents, long deceased, had been only children so there was no family and he had always been terrible at making friends. All he had were acquaintances and co-workers and none of them had cared enough to throw him a retirement party. Although, in fairness, they may have taken him too literally when he had declared he didn't want one. All the money, fame, and adulation from his role as Reginald was never enough to sooth his aching bitterness and loneliness and now even that was gone.

He closed the curtains, tore his gaze from the glass, and reached into the bottom drawer for the first of his only true companions. He set the quart container of blind tiger whiskey, unlabeled and illegally distilled, on the vanity top. He had purchased a case of the fiery rot-gut outside of Gatlinburg, Tennessee a few weeks ago and was, suddenly and to his surprise, down to this last bottle.

He leaned over to reach further back into the same bottom drawer. His fingers curled around the rubber grip of his ancient but well-maintained Ruger LCR .38 Special double-action revolver made from aerospace grade aluminum. This was his other companion and he called her the Gray Lady. Cradling it in both hands with arms extended and pointing the firearm to the side, he pushed the cylinder eject button and, with a flick of the wrist, flipped the cylinder open. All five chambers were filled with +P rounds. Another flick and the cylinder snapped back into place. The Lady was placed next to the blind tiger whiskey.

Reggie looked long and hard at both, sighed deeply. It wasn't that he was overly-tired and weak, that all his energy was spent, that his skin itched terribly and the right side of his abdomen ached continuously, that he was lonely and friendless, that he had no plans or goals for tomorrow, or the next day, or the day after. It was the lifelong inability to make important decisions because of the fear of making the wrong one. And so he sat there, perplexed, unsure of which he would taste first.

M. Kelly Peach is a husband, father of four adult children and grandfather of three grandsons. He enjoys reading, writing, collecting books, baking, and camping. He's been a taco fryer, dishwasher, cook, library aide, maintenance helper, teacher, workforce development professional, supervisor, and, for the State of Michigan, a Project Zero Coordinator, Eligibility Specialist, and Community Resource Coordinator. His Twitter account is @MichaelPeach. He has published essays in *Punchnel's*, *Alternate Hilarities III*, *Mad Scientist Journal Summer Issue 2014*, *Entropy*, and *Woods-N-Water News*, and short stories in *Alternate Hilarities I* and *II*, *Cheapjack Pulp*, *Unsung Stories*, *In Medias Res: Stories of the In-Between*, and *Strangely Funny IV*.

Alone with Gandhari

Gord Sellar

And the wailing chief of the cowherds fled, forlorn and spent,
Speeding on his rapid chariot to the royal city went,
Came inside the city portals, came within the palace gate,
Struck his forehead in his anguish and bewailed his luckless fate.
       — from *The Mahabharata*, trans. Romesh C. Dutt (1898)

She was out there, serene in the mists, waiting for him, and Ron was coming to her. With the whole of his mind, he willed himself to see her: her immense walnut eyes, slightly alien; her long, regal nose with its flaring nostrils; her long, elegant legs.

And then, suddenly, there she was in all her natural glory: no genetic engineering or hormonal tinkering had been performed upon her, and as such, she was a precious rarity. A creature of such loveliness, a sight for bruised and red-veined eyes. She eyed him calmly as he hurried toward her across the field of endless green and softly swaying daisies, under a sky so blue it would have made you weep if only it were real.

A memory of Kenny stirred—that poor, sad, dead glob of pudge he'd once been, that Ron had murdered in an empty field one night near

Alone with Gandhari

Fort Worth with four Brother Ronalds. The ghost of a dead lardass grasping at his spirit's throat, trying to haul itself back up through the greasy lips of oblivion.

Ron ignored it. The remnant artifacts of Kenny Jameson's pathetic life—an army-green trash bag full of oversized clothes and whimpering regrets—had been left to rot in a shallow hole in the ground behind a shopping mall. With Guru Deepak's help, he'd long ago learned how to deal with Kenny's ego, the remnants of the man Ron had been before his rescue. He slowed his pace as he approached Gandhari, savoring the scratchy caresses of the high blue grass against his naked legs.

When he reached her side, he patted her twice upon the hip, with all the gentleness of a tender lover. "*Namasté*, Gandhari. Now, look at me," he said with a smile. "Look at my body." He glanced down at his own taut gut, the thin threads of wasted muscles beneath his somehow-clean skin. He had become somehow translucent, and could see the his own knobby, badly-carved kneecaps, the weary veins in his legs, the clutching bones of his ribcage, and even the curve of his pelvic bones through his patchily tanned, hairless hide.

Gandhari turned her head, lazily surveying his physique. She belched, and a heavenly draught bathed his face. He was suddenly moved by his passion for her, great Gandhari, gods-kissed blindfolded mother of a hundred sons from the Great Book, who had long ago attained her true and perfect form. He touched his lips to her forehead, between her eyes, and in response, she lovingly swished her tail over her back, an ancient gesture that meant nothing but pure bovinity in this world where flies buzzed no more.

Heart swooning, he made his way to her rear, and as he did so, she steadied herself, bracing. Gently, and with the greatest of reverence, he stuck a hand into her, and then another. He pried her open, drew a deep breath, and slid headfirst into the peace of the divine mother-cow's womb.

———————

Within her, there were others. The sounds of breathing and mumbled prayers and mantras. And Guru Deepak, preaching off in the distance, his voice muffled but undeniably musical.

Ron ignored the others. He relaxed, breathing mother Gandhari's life-giving uterine fluids into his lungs, leaning back against the soft, warm walls of her womb. He was alone with Gandhari, within her. He was home, again. Nothing else mattered.

Then she spoke to him. Close by, tender yet clear, it was her womb-voice speaking to him alone, and he dreamed the most loveliest visions: of broken buildings, smoke and flames, and a endless, rising wave of liberation sweeping the earth entire.

———————

"Listen, Kenny," Mr. Paul said to him one day, in the staff room during his lunch break. "I'm gonna have to let you go."

"Why?" Envelopes with little plastic windows filled Kenny's mind. Bills inside them, and sternly worded final notifications. Without Prejudice.

"You really wanna know?"

"Uh... yeah?"

"Because you're a fat fuckin' pig, Kenny," his boss said. "People don't *wanna* see you servin' their french fries and deep-fried, greasy chicken, Kenny. It reminds them of why they *shouldn't* be eating it in the first place. It's bad for our image."

Alone with Gandhari

Kenny wanted to shout, to punch Mr. Paul in the stomach, to tell him to go screw himself, shove the job up his ass sideways. He knew his rights! He didn't have to take this! He wanted to chuck his soda onto Mr. Paul's shirtfront and tell him to ram his shitty job up his skinny little ass. But he just retreated inside himself, and began thinking again about how to check out of hotel butterball.

Pills, Kenny decided, but he lowered his head, and just mumbled his response.

"What?" Mr. Paul sounded defensive, as if he expected a lawsuit or an outburst or something. But Kenny wasn't going to sue. He'd grown accustomed to maltreatment. That was just how fat people lived: obesity was the new leprosy. People even avoided your touch, like it was catching or something.

"Should I finish out my shift?" he asked again, louder. It was a bad time to be out of a job, with talk of another war in the air. Though at least he was too fat to be drafted. They'd never send him to Venezuela, let alone North Korea.

"Nah, just go on home," he said, stealing one of Kenny's fries and shoving it into his mouth. "We'll mail your last paycheck to you."

Kenny nodded, defeated, and turned to leave. *Pills*.

"And Kenny... don't come back here again till you lose a couple of belt notches, you hear me?" Mr. Paul said, half-smirking.

Kenny never did go back there, though it'd be the first place Ron would attack, a few months later.

Meditations always ended, but today, they faded out too soon, and Ron found himself back in the claustrophobic hell of a media helmet that stank and was stuffy with desert heat. No matter how necessary the return to the world was, it always deadened him a little to leave behind the soft electromagnetic massage of the helmet and his brief audience with ultimate reality.

He removed the helmet carefully, wrapping it again in an old patchwork quilt, and rose to stow it for the day. All around him, other Ronalds were doing the same thing. There were so many of them: Mexican, black, gringo like himself, female and male alike. Some were wrapping their helmets, and others, that task completed, were sleepily ruffling their dyed-scarlet afros, slipping into their grungy yellow jumpsuits.

Guru Deepak, shirtless in his golden dhoti, stood beside the storage shelving units in the back of the decrepit U-Haul trailer behind one of the campers. He smiled toothily and mouthed encouragements to them as they stowed the VR gear safely away. To Ron, he said, "Mother Gandhari has blessed you specially," and set his broad hand on Ron's shoulder.

Ron didn't know what to say. He hadn't spoken to Guru Deepak in days. Not out of any animosity: it was just one of his silence kicks, the sort of habit Deepak indeed praised and tended not to interrupt.

"Why?" Ron asked, after a moment's dazed thought.

"Later," Deepak said with a small shrug of his powerful shoulders, and showed him his beautiful white teeth through a grin. They were perfectly straight, a show of dental perfection that could only be divine in nature.

Breakfast always followed meditations, so Ron made his way to the kitchen. A big vat of greenish *dhal* was bubbling in a cookpot on the ground, and a huge tray of breads—*naan*, loaves, buns—sat together in a big assortment. Bean soup again, he moaned inwardly. But immediately, he caught himself, seized his own disappointment, and pinned it to the wall of his mind as one might a live frog for dissection. He jabbed his resentment with harshness he'd once reserved for lily-livered politicians and hardened criminals.

Bless Gandhari, his craving for meat hadn't returned. His self-control was always greater after a few hours in Her womb. A few minutes later, a bowl of dhal and a few hunks of bread in his possession, he sat down in his usual place, among usual faces. "Namasté, Ronald," they all greeted him in something too jumbled to be called unison.

"*Namasté*, Ronalds," he said. "What's up?"

Ron had meant nothing by it, but it seemed to him that, unlike most days, something *was* indeed up. They regarded him with careful, awkward eyes, blinking silent and waiting for someone to spill the proverbial beans.

Finally, the Mexican Ronald spoke up and said, with his familiar, heavy accent: "Guru say something t'you, don't he?"

"How'd all y'all know about that?"

"In Gandhari's womb," the bony, flat-chested Ronald chick whispered, "I heard something. You know how it is."

Ron did. Visions and whispers sometimes came. Prophecies, gleanings of Deepak's wisdom. Burning visions of the future.

"Last time I had a vision like this one..." she said, leaning forward. "Well, there was a Mac Attack coming up soon, and that Ronald, Gandhari said the same words to..." She glanced down into her bowl of *dhal*, dipping a chunk of whole-wheat bread into the slop, and chewed noisily, as if she had no intention of finishing the sentence.

Ron kept his eyes on her as he expertly tore a piece of bread off and used it to spoon up some *dhal* without looking into the bowl.

When she was about to dip her *naan* into her *dhal* again, he hissed, "*What?*"

"Listen," she said. "If you're lucky, you'll be drinking mother Gandhari's pure milk today. *In heaven,*" she added, as if the euphemism hadn't been clear enough, and dropped the bread into her *dhal.* Her eyes softened a little, the tattooed-red tip of her nose wiggling as she sniffed, and with a lowered voice she added, "If you want, we can go out behind the storage sheds and I'll give you a... you know." She jerked a grubby fist up and down suggestively, one gaunt cheek propping outward by her tongue as she gave him a ghastly wink. "Just in case. Nothing more, though. I don't wanna get pregnant before It happens. *He feeds on childrens' minds; they make Him stronger,*" she droned, intoning the familiar mantra that Ronalds chanted to fend off carnal temptation. "But I'll get you off, one last time before..."

"No thanks," Ron said, and filled his mouth with hot, flavorless green bean mush. It wasn't much of an act of will: she wasn't his type, her breath stank, she was missing half her teeth, and anyway, he didn't believe he was going to be a martyr. He'd done nothing to distinguish himself or earn such an honor. And even if Gandhari *had* chosen him to lead a mission, it didn't mean he was going to die.

"Are you sure?" she said and licked her bright-red lips, her eyes slightly narrowed. He realized that she wasn't being generous: she really *wanted* to do it. He wondered how many other martyrs she'd led off the path, the same day they were supposed to drink straight from Gandhari's udder, and sent them spiraling back into the *samsaric* rut of reincarnation and flesh-addiction.

Who hungers for flesh of one kind, hungers for all, went Guru Deepak's motto.

Was it jealousy, that Mother Gandhari always chose men to lead the Mac

Attacks? Or some vestigal human instinct, half-desiccated lust? He imagined the Ronalds he'd admired: those he'd seen shot to death in the parking lots of ghastly eateries, and those whose bodies had been charred by fires or clapped in irons and shipped to reprogramming facilities, their animal bodies trapped and ensouled once again by the System. He imagined himself out behind the storage sheds, or huddled in the cab of a truck, or somewhere behind a clump of bushes, with her rancid breath wafting hot across his skin. Thick, acidic bile scoured its way up his throat.

Stop, he commanded himself, and he stepped back from all of these overwhelming emotions that had welled up within. From a slight mental distance, his envy and desire looked pathetic. His own disgust peered back at him impishly. They had fused, and sang in one voice. But when he looked deeper, he found sorrow and disdain, braided into one single wormlike creature and wriggling within his mind. He looked upon his flat-chested Ronald Sister and abjured that strange sadness-and-dislike emotion, struggling for compassion.

"No thank you," he said with a smile, and admonished her with a mantra of his own. *"After a Single Sip, Only a Big Gulp Can Follow."*

"Yes, true," she said, nodding, and attacked her food. She tried to look relieved, but refused to meet his gaze again the whole meal. That didn't surprise him; what surprised him was that none of the other Ronalds caught his eye again, either.

The first time he had seen a Mac Attack, he'd almost pissed in his size-52 pants. He'd been standing in the usual burger joint when suddenly they'd burst in, yelling through the speakers mounted on the fronts of their gas-masks.

"Killers! Murderers!" they'd screamed, those freaks. They had looked like Holocaust victims done up in soiled yellow clown costumes, red grins tattooed onto their faces, red curly wigs slapped onto their bald crowns. "You're filthy! You're insane!" Even in his panic, he'd thought, *Look who's talking.* He remembered that, the way one remembers being a heartbroken teenager, or remembers the panic of holding a steering wheel for the first time: the memory of another person altogether, was what it now felt like to Ron.

But he hadn't yet become a Ronald, then. He had been a different kind of human. No, not human, either. A man, maybe, but not human. He'd been a mere scraping beast. A herd man. Kenny the flabby herd man.

Seeing the Ronalds in action, he'd seen not their liberation from mediocrity, but only the dirt clinging to their faces, the blood and grime ground into the fabric of their costumes, the dung clinging to their floppy red shoes. They'd been liberated from the trap of ego and identity, and attained McMoksha, but through the thickening haze of the gas bombs they'd set off, he'd stared into their eyes behind their gas-masks and seen only one thing: *crazy.*

Little had he known, as he'd stumbled out the side door, through the parking lot, coughing and sputtering on the fumes, that *he* was the crazy one. He'd staggered past the rear bumper of his second-hand jalopy of a truck, its bumper crusted in consumers' rights bumper stickers with blinking mottoes like: "Hands off my fried chicken!" and, "My lard, my life."

He'd burned the last reserves of his energy hoisting himself up into the seat of his truck, squeezing in sideways, getting his foot onto the gas pedal.

Alone with Gandhari

Still choking and coughing, he'd started the pickup truck's engine, and, not bothering with the seat-belt—it didn't fit him anyway—he'd slammed his foot down onto the accelerator.

He'd managed to cling to consciousness long enough to get down the road and slam his truck into a traffic-light pole in front of a gas station. Someone had already called 911 by then, and when the ambulance had shown up, they'd just given him an injection and a coffee and made him sit by the gas station and wait for the cops to come and taken his statement. They'd even let him drive himself home an hour or two later.

His truck had been seriously dented, but his mind had been damaged far worse. The attack had hit him harder than the last international foreign terrorist attacks all rolled into one. It took him a week before he went to a burger joint again.

No other week in his life had ever felt as much like forever.

"My dear, brave Ronnies!" Guru Deepak declared to the eager assembly of the faithful.

They paused, setting their preparations aside, and turned to face their guru, settling on their backsides in the hot sand. White face-paint set off the black crusts beneath their fingernails, and excited gap-toothed smiles lit up their pimpled, scarred faces.

"Today, we launch a very important assault," Guru Deepak declared, his head wobbling side to side insistently. "All our past struggles have led up to this. Yes, this is very-very important! Today, we end our endless attacks on the lowest levels of the death chains. The world has heard our message, and had many chances to heed it. The willing have already joined us."

"And those who have chosen to ignore us... it is a tragedy, my Ronnies. It is heartbreaking. Every one of you knows what it was like to be a carnivore, to feast on the blood and bodies of poor animals. Every one of you, until you joined us, turned a deaf ear to the screams of murdered beasts suffering in your own flabby bellies. You thought you were punished for it, when being fat was almost a crime, but no punishment ever stopped you. Who aided you? Yes, I did... in Gandhari's name."

Ronald felt a tear in his eye. It all came back to him now, the people had stared at him. Their hissing whispers, as he'd gone by, echoed in his tortured soul. He remembered catching eyes with other fat people, obese women who'd looked at him with those wide, sorrowful eyes. *I know*, their looks had said, and he'd avoided their gaze. He hated those looks. Pious, hopeful pity. He had pitied those women back, who were surely as lonely as he was, but nonetheless he'd seen them as bulbous hags he would never stoop to touching. He'd never made one fat friend, ever. He'd hated fat people with a passion most people never experience in their happy, healthy lives.

And now, he looked down at himself, and he could see the bones within his arms; he could bend and touch his toes without any trouble; he hadn't had a backache in months, though his muscles still twitched and shuddered every once in a while, and some of his teeth were coming loose. He never felt lonely anymore, though he didn't feel the opposite of lonely, either. He wasn't sure, even, what the opposite of lonely *was*.

"It was no sin. Being fat was a symptom. Not of your glands, my Ronnies, for none of you is fat now, and we have not changed your glands. Not of symptom of weakness: you are not weak people, and the world shudders when we attack. It was a symptom of your society. We know what it was a symptom of, don't we?"

Then the Ronnies began to recite the mantra together, Ron's voice one of dozens. They chanted this mantra together whenever a craving for fries or a burger hit one of their group:

Ravenous mouths, ravenous heads,
Devouring bodies and the earth,
The sickness of the living dead,
Eternal death, empty rebirth.

They repeated it over and over, faces turned skyward and eyes closed heavenward. After three, maybe four dozen repetitions, Ron felt a firm hand on his shoulder.

He opened his eyes, and standing above him was Guru Deepak. The Indian gestured with his eyes toward the center of the crowd, from where he'd been speaking, and whispered, "Come on."

Ron rose on wobbly legs and followed him to the elevated platform at the crowd's center, and just as he reached it, a few Ronalds—those in Deepak's inner circle, clown-masked female eunuchs who went about with their beautiful bodies nude, clean and smooth and white as a millionaire's finest dishplates—led a blotchy-coated, thin brown cow out onto the platform. Deepak tried to keep Ron distracted, but he glimpsed a muzzle on her nose, holding her mouth shut. The eunuchs slid it off quickly once they got her onto the platform, and after a few moments, she let out a loud, insistent *moo.*

The chanting stopped. Eyes bloomed slowly open, heads nodded downward from blind sky-gazing, and they caught sight of the cow.

"It is Gandhari!" Deepak hollered, and the Ronalds howled back with ecstatic joy. The cow flicked her tail listlessly, and farted. "She has chosen a Ronald to lead the mission!" he cried out, and Ron felt the guru's hand clap him on the shoulder.

The joyous screams grew louder still as the Ronalds surged toward him and the cow. Their tattooed red mouths and noses, their teary eyes, blurred before Ron, and he turned to the cow. With all his might, he fought the ghostly poison of Kenny's illusions, and willed himself to see not the sickly Jersey cow before him, but instead the true, beautiful, utter Gandhari.

And then it was effortless, seeing ultimate reality: she was standing right there before him, eyes burning with divine love as she chewed her timeless, life-giving cud. She exuded holiness, contentment. The cow radiated ineffable hope.

Ron felt a boundless joy he'd never felt before.

The meeting had been held in a small room in the downtown Fort Worth YMCA. Corpulent men and women had sat in a circle, talking about their addictions. A.A. for the Obese, the counselor had said. It was the only way the hospital had let him go, after he'd failed to kill himself with painkillers one Sunday afternoon.

Ron had found the rules were insulting. A higher power? You had to believe in God to stop pigging out? Ten steps, twelve steps... whatever. That last night at the Y, he'd made up his mind not to come back.

But at the end of the meeting, the counselor, a gaunt Yankee with a shaved head and some kind of certificate from a nothing college in Vermont, had caught his arm and said his name softly. "Kenny," he'd said.

"Yeah?" Kenny had said, trying not to let on that he'd given up on the support group.

"I can see what you're thinking. That this group isn't going to help you."
"Naw, it ain't that." Kenny had been like that, then—so terrified of the truth:

frightened to say it, frightened even to acknowledge it. "I'm just having an off day, and..."

"No, you're right to think it. This group *isn't* going to help you. But I know someone who can. I know someone who can *free* you. You know, I used to be..." He paused, a droplet of sweat on his brow sliding softly down in the harsh fluorescent light.

"What?"

The group facilitator had reached into his wallet, and pulled out a picture of an enormous man. A man so heavy it was difficult to imagine him walking, seated at a cheap diner table with a burger meal set in front of him, smiling.

"That's what I look like five years ago," he'd said.

"Well, lucky you," Kenny had said, eager to flee his chance at liberation. "So for you it was just diet. Not glandular, or..."

Kenny had tried to push past him, but the man had stopped him, and said, "You know, people have glandular problems all over the world. But there is *nobody* this fat in Myanmar. There's almost nobody this fat in Uzbekistan, either." He lowered his voice when he said the names of those countries, looking around anxiously. What, was he paranoid too? As if any government department—even Homeland Security—would plant someone in a fatties' support group! "It's an excuse, and you know it."

"So what am I supposed to do?"

The guy lowered his voice a lot, then, practically to a whisper, as he suggested, "Why not come with me and find out?"

Kenny had noticed a few locks from the red wig in the backseat of the man's car, just barely peeking out from under a magazine, but he hadn't put two and two together until much later. He'd been too busy feeling mortified at how the car's seatbelt hadn't fit around his torso.

"Don't worry," his counselor had said, nodding in that encouraging way he always did. "I've been there myself. It'll get better. I promise," he'd promised, turning his head to scan the parking lot one more time. Then they'd pulled out just a little too fast and sped off into the night.

———

"What are you doing here?" the man in the suit screamed.

Ron smiled silently, crossing the room slowly and carefully while the man scrambled with the drawers of his desk. Glass crunched beneath his feet, and somewhere in the building, an alarm wailed. He could hear the fluttering of bodies in motion, and terrified cries outside the man's office. Fools, resisting the Ronalds who were trying to save them. He ignored all of that, and stared into the man's eyes.

This was the right guy. His face had been burned into Ron's mind during his last meditation session, within Gandhari's womb. Ron raised his taser.

The man drew a pistol out from a drawer, and had it halfway up to Ron's face when the needles slammed into his chest, through his fine tailored shirt.

"Don't," Ron said, a tiny smile curving within the thick red smile tattooed into the skin of his face.

The man pulled the trigger. Nothing happened. He'd panicked, forgotten about the safety. That was enough time for Ron. He thumbed a button, and pain swept down the taser wires, through the needles and into the man.

Who then howled.

"Drop it," Ron ordered him.

The man didn't obey. His clumsy hands fiddled with the gun, and then he tried to raise it toward Ron again.

Ron increased the voltage, and the man howled again,louder, dropping the gun involuntarily. Ron's heart flooded with sorrow and sympathy.

That such a powerful minion of the death-chains could fall to the ground and suffer, writhing pathetically—he needed to be liberated as much as anyone.

Ron slipped a paper bag over the man's head and hauled him up, still shivering, to his unsteady feet.

"Congratulations," he said. "You've just been rescued."

The back of the van was crammed with people, their ruddy-cheeked faces terrified. They weren't fat, like the death-eaters Ron had seen walking the streets earlier in the day, on the way to the offices. These were kind of people whose daily schedules allowed for an exercise regimen, for occasional liposuction when necessary, for dietary restrictions. They could afford to eat well, and...

Ron sighed. He had to admit it to himself: they probably were not addicted as he had been, when his name had been Kenny. They would be almost impossible to liberate. They liked living in this evil, awful world they'd built.

"Where are we going?" shouted the CEO from under his paper bag.

"This is just routine inspection procedure, sir," Ron said. "We want to see the state of your cattle."

"You're crazy! You asshole! We can't go to every..."

"We don't *need* to," snapped Ron. "Y'all got an indoor ranch set up under San Marcos, don't you?"

"What? How do you...?" One of the men reached for the paper bag on his head.

The wiry, half-Japanese Ronald chick from Oklahoma slapped his hand, and in her high-pitched voice, she said, "Don't even try it, Mac!"

All the other Ronnies burst out into laughter at her clever pun.

"You'd be surprised how much we know, Mr. Dalton," Ron said once they had stopped guffawing. He let the man stew in that the rest of the way out to San Marcos.

If you want to imagine the future they want to build, Guru Deepak had preached once, *imagine a boot stamping on a cow's face, forever.* Ron could see the boot before him, a big black industrial jackboot made from cow's leather. It was stomping and stomping, brutal and incessant.

He comforted himself with another Guru Deepak's teachings: I am a cow. You are a cow. We are all cows. We have been, and will again be, cows. We shall graze on green fields, and somewhere, sometime else, we are cows and bulls grazing on green fields. There is a calm and beautiful cow within every one of us. *Namasté:* the cow within me greets and salutes the cow within you.

That was the message of Guru Deepak, the whole of it, the heart and soul of it, and it comforted Ron as the van rolled out along the highway towards horrors unimaginable.

———

The people had met him with smiles and encouraging looks.

"My name is Kenny, and I'm a fast-food addict," he'd said. They'd all sat there quietly, listening to his story. Which had been nothing special, just extra portions and aunts and uncles telling him to finish this or that so they wouldn't have to take it home. School dances sat skipped out on, and the looming threat of diabetes. Bottles of cola every day, and the antidepressant effects of fries, burgers, desserts, and more burgers. How he'd finally tried to kill himself, and found he was too fat to die on a mere half-bottle of painkillers.

They'd smiled and nodded, listened generously. He'd felt weird telling them this, all these slim people, but they'd looked at him with what had felt, for the first time in years, like genuine respect.

"So," he'd finished off, "I'm looking at all of you, and you're all so slim. Skinny, even. I kinda can't believe that y'all used to be big like me. But that gives me hope. I can change, you know?"

They'd clapped, and one of them, an Indian wearing a long golden shirt, had nodded as the clapping petered out and the others had looked at him. *Dude looks like Gandhi*, Kenny thought to himself for a moment. *But with muscles and more hair.*

"Oh, yes, Kenny," he'd said with a wide, reassuring smile, his head nodding sideways. "I can help you change yourself. If you want it badly enough. But changing yourself isn't enough. If we want to change ourselves, we must also change the world."

Kenny had remembered, then the image he'd seen in the mirror a few days before, puke all down his undershirt, on that day he'd tried to die. Sagging man-tits under his thin yellow-stained undershirt, useless nipples as wide as silver dollars. All those eyes on him, the years and years of eyes focusing the way they do when people look at lizards and snakes. Then there had risen ache inside him, deep down at his core. He'd wanted to sleep with someone before he died. Someone real. Someone shaped like a woman —like a cello, not a pear or a watermelon. He'd wanted to run again, in this life.

"Sign me up," Kenny had said, and then he noticed that one of them was fidgeting with a hypodermic needle in her hand.

Ron inhaled deeply. The bovoid stench was incredible, like a million tons of rank milk and blood and the faintest hint of corn-syrup in the air. Sweet, not disgusting the way he'd expected.

The hairless thing's meters-long torso hung in a tickle-harness, for all the world like an immense caterpillar shuddering reflexively from the automated stimulation. Dozens of "legs" hung floppily from its side, squirming occasionally. They looked more like enormous fins of boneless meat, each bearing only a tiny black nail—the vestige of a hoof—at its tip. Stumps of other legs, still regenerating from the last meat-harvest, were visible.

Food and waste plumbing penetrated every natural orifice and a few artificial ones, as well. A series of udders, a dozen at least, hung from its underside, through the netting of the harness that suspended it. Pipe-feeds attached to each one. Ron could not tell whether the end he was looking at was the mouth or the ass, because the heads had been engineered out of these beasts. Superfluous, brains and faces. Not even eyes. Just tubes going in one end and out the other.

"This *isn't* a cow," Ron said. "It shits liquid fuel and it pisses sugar water and secretes two hundred liters of milk a day. It regrows its... *legs*... a hundred times before they give out. It has, what, sixteen or twenty wombs? And not one brain. This thing is *not* a cow."

"Yes it is," Mr. Dalton said, his dull eyes defiant. "According to the FDA..."

"Fuck the FDA! Screw 'em in the throat with a chainsaw!" Ron howled. "*Look* at that thing... it doesn't even look like a land animal!"

"What the hell do you think *you* look like?" Dalton snapped, and then winced in sudden fear.

Ron wiggled the tip of his tattooed-red nose and jammed one finger of his grimy white-gloved hand into Dalton's chest. "Look who's talking," he said.

Alone with Gandhari

From the corner of his eye, he glimpsed a movement. A ranch worker had lunged at him with a rifle. The gunshot blast sent all the hostages flat to the floor, Dalton included, but a thick, white-gloved hand clubbed the rancher flat onto the floor, unconscious.

Ron turned to New York Ronald—a tall guy with an Italian-looking face under his white paint and clownface tattoos. He was the one who'd taken out the would-be hero, and he kicked the gun from the rancher quickly, before turning to see if Ron was okay.

"Thanks, Ronald," he barked. His savior acknowledged it with a nod.

The ranch-monsters hung row on row, oblivious in their harnesses, deaf as fingers and thumbs cut from a body and thrown to the ground. Looking upon them, rage boiled up within Ron. He could feel Gandhari within him, weeping for the fate of her brothers and sisters, these perverted things that should have been cows.

While some of the Ronalds chained up the farm-workers and office slugs together in manacles, Ron turned to his second in command—a big black Ronald who was blind in one eye—and muttered, "Little change of plans, Ronald. We're bringing the boss man with us…"

"You sure, Ronald?" Worry was visible in the man's sunken, bloodshot eye.

"Yeah, no problem. Let's do this, everyone. Hurry up!"

The Ronalds howled, hoisting their jerry cans and chanting all the way.

An hour later, the silent writhing of bovoid horrors aflame still screaming through their minds, the Ronalds shoved their prisoners out of the back of their truck, still chained together, out into the desert heat. They begged to be dropped off in the city, but the Ronalds knew better than that: Homeland Security—or, well, someone hired temporarily by DHS, anyway—would be on top of them within ten minutes of the first phone call. Faraway in the distance, thick black smoke seethed up out of the ground and poisoned the desert air.

"We'll drop your phones off a few miles up the road, beside the road. Someone will come and get you," Ron said, and the door slammed, leaving them on the highway like ghosts in the sandy nothingness, the towering shadows of wind turbines slashing across the road behind them. There they left them.

All but Dalton, whom they drugged and shoved into a corner of the van.

"We can *save* him," Ron said, his eyes fervid, lit by the remembered flames, now distant. Eyes dark with the smoke that filled the distant air. Eyes gleaming unnaturally with a bloody passion. The others said nothing, but their eyes avoided him as the truck tore down the dirt roads, back to camp, shaking them as they sat silent, waiting.

Guru Deepak streaked the thick red *pooja* paste up between Gandhari's eyes, to the top of her head. The assembled Ronalds tossed flowers into the air, adorning her with necklaces of blossoms.

She mooed.

Dalton sat nearby, handcuffed. He oozed disdain. From a distance, Ron had watched Deepak argue with him until, suddenly, the shouting had cooled and Deepak had left the man sitting in the sand.

Ron's hope refused to wither. A man like Dalton coming into the fold would be an absolute coup, a portent of worldwide victory. His gaze drifted back to Gandhari, who was being led close to him, so he cast his blossoms up into the air and cried out in joy and boundless, ecstatic praise.

––––––––––

An hour later, he huddled down to the floor in Guru Deepak's private trailer.

"It's alright," he said.

"What?" Guru Deepak wore an incongruous frown upon his face.

"It's alright. I didn't do it for any reward. I just was inspired... by Her—Mother Gandhari. I knew in my heart that she wanted him brought to our camp."

"Really," Deepak muttered. It wasn't a question. Ron carefully searched his guru's face, surprised, until Deepak snapped, "How do *you* know what Gandhari wants? How do you know what *I* want?"

Ron gasped, panic shivering alive in his guts. Had he *really* made a mistake?

"I... I just felt... when I saw all those... things..."

"I know," Deepak said, suddenly quiet, but very, very cold. "I know who you are, Kenny," he said, his eyes narrowing.

"What? No... I'm not Kenny anymore..."

"You think I'm so naïve?" Deepak asked, a little harshly. Ron's heart began to thump.

"What are you *talking* about?"

"You're the fifth plant they've sent," Deepak said, his accent much less pronounced than usual, and his scowl luminous. "I thought you bunch might start finding some other way to spend all those bloody taxes. Don't play dumb with me. You know very well how Dalton's involved. What bringing him here is going to jeopardize. You know *exactly* what you're doing." Deepak's accent had disappeared, and with it his beatific smile. The man looked like any old business captain, suddenly, even in his long golden kurta and brand-name sandals.

"Involved? What? What are you... I don't understand, Guru," Ron said, and he dropped to his knees. "Please... whatever I've done..." Tears streamed down his cheeks, and he touched his master's feet.

Guru Deepak stared at him for a moment, cautiously, and then his expression brightened. "Could you really not be...?" he asked. "I want you to go meditate in Mother Gandhari's womb."

"Thank you," Ron whispered, touching Deepak's feet again, and he hurried out of the trailer to the trunk containing the VR gear.

As he slid headfirst into the great cow's womb, Ron's heart was full of fear and confusion. He trembled in the darkness, and she said nothing to him for what felt like many days. The silent darkness was bisected by the pinprick sensation of an intravenous feed being inserted into the faraway arm of Ron's faraway body, and still, he waited, as desert heat grew and subsided, like tides on the shore.

When she finally spoke to Ron, his faraway body—all but abandoned, that stinking flesh—was stretched out across the dusty ground, the helmet too heavy to support any longer. What she whispered to him was terrifying. Promises of plagues. Deadly cows wandering, dazed, through the smoldering ruins of shopping malls, speaking a language no human ears had ever heard, exhaling deadly contagion scented as sweet as wildflowers. Millions of their two-legged oppressors dead and left to rot, the meat in their bellies burning its way through them, unleashing wracking, fatal sicknesses. It was the end of the human world, the end of that long, hard, ceaseless fouling of the earth.

Alone with Gandhari

It had come already, she told him, this end. It could never, ever be undone, she told him. She was elated, and his exhausted body bubbled with glee, knowing the plague would claim him, soon, too.

Shanti, shanti, he reminded himself. *Peace, peace.* Rebirth, he knew, would eventually come. He meditated, and he prayed, and it felt as if yet more months passed. Distant voices muttered somewhere over the virtual horizon, all of them too faint for the words to reach him. Rumors of a war. The gossip of an enemy, of government agents shouting, searching his body, rifling through the dreams in Gandhari's womb.

Ron desired nothing more than to be born, in his next life, as a calf. Not as a man, at least: as something other—finer—than a human being. He yearned for his true, eternal form. To be a silent bull grazing the weeds of the remade earth. The image sang to him of the voices of choirs, the dung of the world, worms in the soil. An endless chorus of low, undulating moos.

And at the far end of the that eternally warm and wet silence, a ripple surged through the womb shrouding his body—still the body of a man, though he was certain it would be transformed at any moment into his true four-legged form—and with a gentle quiver, he was pushed from dark, warm, sludgy comfort toward the dry dust and cold, once again out into the frightening nighttime of the world.

Gord Sellar is a Canadian writer who has lived in South Korea almost continuously since 2002.

He was a finalist for the John W. Campbell Award for Best New Author in 2009, and his work has appeared in many magazines and anthologies including *Clarkesworld, Asimov's Science Fiction, Analog Science Fiction & Fact,* and has been translated to a number of foreign languages.

In collaboration with his wife Jihyun Park, he has also contributed cotranslations of a number of Korean speculative fiction stories to *Clarkesworld, Readymade Bodhisattva* and a forthcoming collection of the works of South Korean author Bo-young Kim. He also wrote the screenplay for the award-winning *The Music of Jo Hyeja*, South Korea's first Lovecraftian film adaptation.

You can find him at gordsellar.com or on Twitter as @gordsellar.

Bingo

Andreas Hort

Their screams cut through the night. Crouching behind a bush, Bingo heard them sprint through the forest toward him, their voices and footsteps growing louder. He had picked a spot under the thinnest tree crowns in the area to make sure that enough moonlight shone through to reveal his clown makeup when the time would come.

A movement behind the silvery light, in the darkness. The screams sounded much closer now. Bingo guessed two boys and a girl. If there were more, they were probably dead. Bingo had no doubt the kids had tried to explore the abandoned circus tent at the edge of the forest; the alleged residence of Lanky the Grinning Clown.

This is it, thought Bingo. *This is your moment. Smile. And look heroic. Show them a real clown.*

"Help!" It was the girl. "Somebody help! Please!"

Your moment.

They were no more than thirty feet away.

Twenty-five...

Twenty...

Bingo

He straightened up and walked from behind the bush until the silvery moonlight fell on his face. At the same moment, the three teenagers darted into the light and came to a stop a few feet in front of Bingo.

I was right, thought Bingo. *Two boys and a girl.*

Their clothes were caked in mud and blood, their faces covered with shallow, bleeding scratches, their eyes large and filled with terror, and as they stared at Bingo, they grew larger.

Poor kids, thought Bingo with sympathy.

He smiled.

They screamed.

"Another clown!" shrieked the girl.

"Run," said Bingo in a deep voice he hoped was heroic. "I'll protect you!"

At first, he wasn't sure they heard him over their own screams, but then they dashed off into the bushes.

"Two clowns!" he heard the girl shriek. "There's two fucking clowns!"

There was a rustle of leaves, then another movement in the darkness, and Bingo's heart leaped into his throat when he saw a humanlike figure approaching—only it seemed too tall, too slender, too... lanky.

A shiver ran down his spine. There was a sinking feeling in his stomach.

I shouldn't have come. I'm going to die.

A shoe, a size-seventeen brown shoe, poked out of the darkness and stepped into the moonlight. The leg that followed was covered with black and white stripes, and seemed at least four feet long.

The other leg emerged from the darkness, followed by a narrow body in a red suit and a red bow tie over a green shirt. The being's slender arms ended at its knees, and in one of the hands it was holding an axe. Its handle was long, its head dripping blood. Bingo knew from the legends that Lanky liked using an axe. The only thing he liked using more were his teeth.

Bingo looked up, up, where a pair of large yellow eyes stared down at him out of a white face. The red lips were twisted into a wide, toothy grin.

"You're him," said Bingo in a quivering voice. "You're Lanky the Grinning Clown."

Lanky let out a giggle and nodded. He towered over Bingo, all seven feet and at least six inches of him, and Bingo felt a scream clawing up his throat.

Don't! Remember why you're here! Remember! Remember!

And he did.

He remembered the feeling of happiness and relief when a circus accepted him as the new clown at the age of twenty. He felt home. All he had ever wanted was to bring smiles to people's faces, and then he could.

He remembered the news, the movies, the urban legends. He remembered the audience grow more and more silent with each performance, their smiles thinning, their eyes filling with fear, their children crying, them all leaving, shooting fearful glances and hateful glares over their shoulders, aimed at Bingo standing in the center of the ring and wondering why they didn't like him anymore. He just wanted to make them laugh and feel happy, and they despised him for it.

"I'm sorry, Bingo," said George Barnes, who was the circus owner, a fair man Bingo liked almost as a friend. "I really am. People just don't like clowns anymore. After all those psychos and movies and urban legends... They're afraid of you. They just..." He sighed, looking at Bingo with sincere sadness. "They don't want to see you anymore. I'm sorry, but we have to let you go. I'm really sorry."

Bingo knew perfectly well the two boys and the girl hadn't run away because he told them to. They ran away from him.

And it's his fault, he thought, glaring at Lanky. *Another urban legend. Another psycho. Another freaky clown story.*

Lanky raised the axe over his head and brought it down. Bingo jumped aside and the blade missed his shoulder by inches before sinking into the ground. Bingo reached into his back pocket and pulled out a revolver. Lanky raised the axe again and swung at Bingo's head. Bingo jumped back, feeling the air caress the skin on his neck as the axeblade whooshed past. He cocked the hammer of the revolver, aimed at Lanky the Grinning Clown's heart, and pulled the trigger.

There was a bang, the gun kicked in Bingo's hand, and a fountain of blood gushed out of Lanky's neck, spraying Bingo's face, stinging in his eyes, blinding him.

He shot again. Lanky didn't make a sound. Had he hit him?

He backed away, wiping blood from his eyes. His ears were ringing. Despite the cold weight of the revolver in his hand, he felt exposed. He was aware of every inch of his body as he waited for a heavy axeblade to bite into his flesh.

A heavy axeblade... or sharp teeth.

He shuddered.

He heard a soft humming sound and breeze slid across his face. He opened his eyes and squinted, trying to make out the blurry shapes in front of him. He had no doubt Lanky was swinging at him, from left to right, from right to left, like the madman that he was.

"Aww, Lanky is angry!" Bingo shouted mockingly, like a kindergarten bully, and it felt good to say it that way, it felt good to piss the motherfu—

His heel hit something and he stumbled and lost his balance. He landed on his back in a bush, twigs scratching his cheeks and neck. Lanky was coming at him, blood streaming out of his neck and chest, turning his shirt red and blending it together with the suit—but he was coming. He lifted the axe high above his head.

Bingo raised his revolver and aimed. "Fuck Stephen King!" he yelled and fired. Lanky winced as blood spurted out of his shoulder, and he stepped back.

"Fuck John Wayne Gacy!"

Another bang and Lanky backed away even more, blood streaming out of the hole in his stomach. Lanky didn't seem to mind. He held the axe high above his head, ready to bring it down. His bulging eyes were fixed on Bingo, and he kept grinning. He seemed happy. He seemed to be enjoying himself.

I'll give you something to enjoy.

Lanky started forward. Bingo aimed at his neck.

"And most of all, fuck you!"

He squeezed the trigger. There was a bang and the gun kicked back in his hand. Lanky's eye turned into a black hole. A stream of dark liquid flowed out, down his face and over the grin. The axe fell from his grip. His head tilted backward and his body dropped face up to the ground.

Silence fell, interrupted only by Bingo's heavy breaths.

He scrambled to his feet, took two steps, and looked down at the corpse of Lanky the Grinning Clown.

I killed a person.

The thought came suddenly, and he dismissed it right away. He had killed a monster.

The air carried the acrid stench of blood and gunpowder. Bingo's ears kept ringing, the scratches on his face and neck burned, and his fingers and palm were sore from shooting.

I'll get used to it with time, he thought. He realized he had only shot five times.

He aimed at Lanky's other eye.

"Just a precaution," he mumbled and pulled the trigger.

The earth above Lanky's head exploded.

"Shit." Bingo sighed and glanced at the gun. "I'll have to get better at this."

And I will. There's a lot of work to do. A lot of urban legends to kill. A reputation of a whole profession to fix.

All he needed to do was to show them a real clown. Show them that most clowns were good, and that some of them fought the bad ones.

"There's a clown!" called a deep male voice.

Someone punched him in his lower back, and his first thought was that the boys came back to beat him up. Then a bang reached his ears, and he knew he hadn't been punched; he'd been shot.

No, he thought, panic rising within him. *Not yet. This can't be it! I didn't show them!*

His vision blurred, the ground swayed under his feet, then he felt his body collapse, his face hitting the dirt hard.

"Be careful, Jim! These guys don't stay down for long!"

"Cover me!"

Heavy footsteps were approaching, crushing twigs on the way.

"The second clown's here, too!" called Jim. He sounded very close. Maybe five feet away. "He's dead!"

"You sure?"

"He has a hole in his eye big enough that you could use him as a mini-golf course! He ain't getting up, Donnie."

The steps reached Bingo. A hand gripped his shoulder and turned him around on his back. It hurt a little.

A black man in a blue police uniform towered over him, pointing a gun right at his face.

Coldness spread over him, as if he was being lowered into a bathtub filled two hours ago. His muscles felt like jelly, and his eyelids were heavy. His vision grew more and more blurry, and it took effort to talk, like using an untrained muscle for the first time in years. "I... I killed... him. I... killed Lanky."

Jim the cop glanced at Lanky's corpse, then somewhere beside Bingo's body, probably at the revolver. Was he still holding it or did it lie next to him? He couldn't feel his hands.

"Shit," muttered Jim. He lowered his gun and knelt down beside Bingo. "You saved those kids?"

"...yes."

"Shit." Jim turned over his shoulder. "Donnie, go back to the car and call an ambulance! Now!"

Bingo's eyelids felt oh so heavy, and he couldn't wait to close his eyes and let the sleep take him away from the cold and the pain and the hatred of the world—but there was one more thing he had to say.

"Not all... clowns... are... bad."

"I know." He felt Jim's hand on his shoulder, giving him a gentle, reassuring squeeze. "I know that now."

Bingo sighed as relief washed over him, flushing away the fear and the bitter grievance, leaving only peace, and a little worry, but all he could do now was have faith in the wronged clowns of the world. He let his eyelids close as sleep took him away, away into a warmer, softer place, which slowly dissolved into nothing, and so did he.

He was dead minutes before the ambulance arrived. He had a smile on his face, and the people present didn't find it terrifying at all. In fact, they thought it was quite a nice smile.

Bingo

Andreas Hort resides in the northern part of the Czech Republic. When he's not earning his daily bread working physically oriented jobs, he writes and takes steps toward his goal to move to an English-speaking country. In his free time he works out, reads for pleasure and education, and listens to old drunks' life stories at bus stops on rainy days. His works have been published in several anthologies.

Freckles

Kathleen Palm

Time to face it.

Face *him*.

The stripes on my pants waver as my leg bounces, the yellow, green, and purple lines locked in an epic battle. My white gloves bunch and wrinkle as I curl my fingers against the plain brown couch. The therapist's office is quiet. Shelves of books silently judge. Two empty cushions sit next to me, uncaring. Even though the digital clock makes no sound, the tick-tock of time pulses in my mind. Warm light slides over the ivory walls, but the brightness doesn't reach me.

"I was happy to get your call." The voice, solid, calm. The therapist sits across from me, her elbows resting on the padded arms of the green chair.

Doc—that's what I call her—gives her glasses a tiny push up her nose. She has a name, only after a month of sessions, of talking to her three times a week, I can't remember it. Her foot swings. The frayed hem of her jeans sway.

"Sorry, it's so late, Doc." I gaze out one of the large windows, the light of the sun almost gone. But I couldn't wait. I couldn't stay locked at home with him, with the blood.

Freckles

"Did you just come from another party? You must get a lot of work. I always see you in costume."

"Yeah...a party." There used to be parties. Freckles the Clown was sought after in the world of streamers and balloons. "So many kids." I used to make them happy, make them smile and laugh.

Until their laughter turned on me.

Until my joy decayed into sadness.

Until anger crept through my veins.

Then *he* invaded my life, my mind.

The cold buzz of his thoughts claw at the edges of my brain. My hands shake as I swat at the fringe of the wig at my ears.

"After talking last time," Doc says, shifting in her seat, "I was afraid I wouldn't see you again, so what brings you in?"

Afraid. She doesn't understand fear. But here, this room, this couch. A safe place. That's what Doc says. My oversized black shoes tap on the green rug covered with sweeping spirals. "You're right," I whisper. "I know you're right."

"Right about what, Ja—"

"Doc, please!"

She tucks straight, brown hair behind her ear. "Of course, I'm sorry. Right about what, Freckles?"

I glance at the door, a white shield, though I'm unsure it's strong enough to keep him out. "To face him. I have to face him."

"The man behind the mask?"

"Yes." I tug at my shirt, bright and yellow. A happy shirt for Freckles, now tainted by a stain hidden under my jacket. I reach for my face. Seven freckles dot my cheeks. Seven black spots. Seven. I stop myself before I touch them. "I...I don't want to be this way."

"Why now? When I suggested you take action last time, you were... upset.

You—"

"Ran away. I ran away."

"So why now? What happened?"

The blood happened. I stare at my gloved-hands, remembering the mess, remembering the scrubbing. I flex and curl my fingers. "Because he...what he did..."

"What did he do?" She scoots to the edge of her seat. Maybe interested. Maybe uncertain.

Something awful. Something horrible. Something I won't tell her. I never tell her.

She should be afraid.

I pull the gloves off. My leg stops thrumming up and down, up and down. For a moment, I am still. I am calm.

For a moment.

A shudder jerks across my shoulders, shattering the composure. A serenity I don't want. Flipping my jacket open, I shove my thumbs under my suspenders, happy purple suspenders, and run my hands up and down. As if the action will make him go away. For I heard him. I heard the hiss of his breath, the intent of his heart. "Maybe this isn't a good idea." I tug on my gloves, my trembling hands making it difficult to work my fingers back into their places.

Doc sits back, her face twisted with concern and thought. "It's up to you. It's okay to not be ready to face him."

Ready? My chin hits my chest as I stare at my hands, the blue strands of my wig falling over my cheeks. Cheeks with seven freckles. Hands covered in blood. I pinch the finger of my glove. "One step at a time."

My gloves fall to the floor. A shadow cuts through my thoughts, sharp and cold. I shake off the shiver that oozes up my spine as the struggle of wanting to be free and needing to hide begins.

Freckles

I tug the blue fuzz from my head. The wig joins the gloves and I run my hands over my hair, short and prickly. I sit up, straighten my shoulders. A crack sounds from my neck as I tilt my head one way then the other, aware of the door, the way out.

"Freckles?"

The voice seeps into my mind, like a light in the dark. Yes. Freckles. Not the person under the mask. Not him. My shoulders slump as I drop my gaze to the swirls on the rug, like vortexes waiting to swallow me. He's strong. I want to be stronger, but what if I'm not?

"Freckles? Are you okay?"

Wiggling my fingers, I test that they're mine, because I hear him.

"Freckles?" Worry lines Doc's green eyes, outlined by dark rimmed glasses.

"What?"

Doc sits at the front of her chair, her fingers playing with the chain hanging around her neck. "What's going on?"

Such a pretty neck.

Panic runs through me like a million swords. "It's him." I reach for my wig. To put it on. To silence him. To lock him away.

"No, it's you."

Me. A part I hide. A part I hate. A part I dread.

"No. Leave the wig there. You don't need it."

The urge to grab it and place it on my head is almost overwhelming, I curl my fingers away from the blue strands.

"Why don't you take off your jacket?" Doc's face holds hope, encouragement.

"Sure." I nod, fighting the knowledge that this is wrong. Even though, my body quakes, I slide free of the polka dot-covered jacket, one arm at a time. A bit of armor gone. My mask a shield, only it doesn't hold him in.

More and more he runs free. But maybe I can defeat him. Stop him. I toss the jacket over the wig on the floor.

I can be free.

"Good! How do you feel?" Doc pushes her glasses up again, her eyes alight with promise.

My hands tight fists of worry, I push my hands under my suspenders, setting my shoulders free of the restraints. I roll my head from side to side and tug my shirt tails from my waistband. "Strong."

And scared. I tap my feet on the floor, large shoes flopping, and run my hands over my thighs. Because of the pounding of his heart. Because of the sinister nature of his thoughts. Because of the growing need.

His need.

My need.

My feet shake and wiggle as I fumble to untie the laces, until a speck of red lingering under my fingernail catches my eye. I pause to pick the spot free and stare at it on my fingertip, a fragment of terror sitting on my skin, a leftover fleck of a dark moment. My shoes flap and bounce as I stare, petrified of the shadows in the past and the blackness waiting in the future.

"Freckles?"

I glance up at Doc's eyes wrinkled with concern, then back at the dried flake of blood.

"Are you okay? Do you want to keep going?"

"Do I want...?" No. I don't. I don't want to face the person under the mask. I hide him with a smile and goofy laugh.

Because he does bad things. He didn't always. But he does now.

His pulse pounds in my chest. His thoughts fight to strangle mine.

I'm not stronger.

Freckles

"No. No. No." I press my hands to my head, fingers digging into my skin as if I can grab him and yank him out, evict him. When I pull my hands away, the streak of white on my shaking fingers whispers of a crack in my defense.

My feet still, soles set on the floor, I flick the speck of blood from my finger. I bend to reach my shoes, and my persistence unravels the strings. One shoe then the other thump onto the carpet. The bright stars cover my socks with twinkling happiness, so I strip them off and toss them on top of the pile of clothes. A pile of me.

"Freckles?"

Freckles. I feel his battle to hide me. I run my tongue along my bottom lip, tasting the spice of fright. My bare toes press into the rug, soft and warm. I glance at the window, flexing my fingers and rolling my shoulders. The light of day completely gone, the darkness beyond turns the window into a mirror. The white face stares back at me, his face. Yet not completely white, not anymore. I'm there, peering through the cracks.

His screams of alarm press at the boundary of me.

But I am stronger.

"How are you feeling?" Doc places her pen and paper on the table beside her as she shifts forward, feet planted ready to stand. "Actually...is that blood on your shirt? Are you hurt?"

I shift my gaze to the dark stain. "Hurt? No, but..." A chuckle turns to panic that inches along my quivering arm as my hand hovers over the dark splatter.

Panic becomes a frightened cry.

I stand and force my fingers into fists. A flash of white in the window, and I turn to glare at my face...*his* face. High arched eyebrows. A red grin. And freckles. Seven. A shout of rage silences the fear as I drag my fingers down my cheeks.

Doc stands, approaching. "Freckles? What is it?" Her voice calm, hands outstretched in understanding.

"It's him." He's winning.

"We talked about this. The person under the mask is you."

I shake my head as if to rid myself of the invasion of his thoughts and emotions. "No." My reflection sways as I look at the window. The mask that keeps him at bay is smeared, broken. The clean white shield now cracked. I stare at my fingers, coated with white, then wipe them over the splatter of blood on my shirt as if wanting to paint it over, erase it. "He does bad things."

And I can't stop him.

"What could you have possibly done? You make people smile."

I did. The clothes, the face paint, remain, not a costume, but armor.

And now it's gone. He's loud. He's angry.

A sob fills my throat.

I step to the window, swiping my shirt sleeve down my face.

The blackness of horror washes over my thoughts.

Again, my sleeve erases more of the mask.

There he is, lurking under the red grin.

Again.

My true face revealed. The face of power. The face of revenge. The face of action.

"Freckles?"

Strong. Free. I spin, facing her. "Don't."

My hands close around her throat. "Call me."

I squeeze. "Freckles."

Her fingers claw at mine. Her mouth moves trying to take in needed air. Her eyes blink in disbelief, in terror.

"You never helped him, you know. That stupid frightened clown."

Freckles

Doc's feet thud on the floor. Her fingernails leave red welts on my skin. Her struggle weakens, then stops. Life leaves her eyes. I release her, and she crumples in a heap next to giant shoes, a blue wig, and colorful jacket.

The anger subsides, and my body trembles. I flex my fingers and wave my hands wanting to forget the feel of her skin, of her fading pulse. *He* lurks in the window. His face. His smile. Dread descends like a boulder, dropping from a cliff. Shoulders shaking with my sobs, I run to the pile on the floor. I don't look at Doc as I step around her form. Can't look at what he's done...again. I slam the wig on my head and shove my arms in my jacket. I struggle with my socks, the world blurred by tears.

I grab my bag and dig for the final piece of my armor.

Paint and sponge in hand, I rush to the window, slapping the color on my skin. Stroke after stroke, I hide him. I force him behind the mask of good, of light. Though there's nothing good or light about him... about me.

Because he'll never be gone.

Lip trembling, with a final swipe I finish covering my skin with white. Hands shaking, I draw a red smile, the wavering line surrounds my frown with a lie. My knees buckle, but I fight to stand. My stomach churns, but I swallow the bile as I paint on sweeping, happy brows. Finally, I add black dots. A tear falls with each.

Eight now.

Eight.

<hr>

Kathleen Palm haunts her 100-year-old house with her family, Harry Potter wands, and Stephen King book collection. Writing short stories is a passion, possibly an obsession, that fills time between crafting dark, creepy, and fantastical young adult and middle-grade novels. She can be found reading, sharing her love of horror on *The Midnight Society* blog, chatting with friends on Twitter, and spreading light through her love of the dark.

Clowns on the Run

Daniel Scott White

The road crossed over the river by way of a two-lane bridge. Emmett stuck his head out the window and leaned over. It looked a long way down to the water, a long way down for nothing.

The cattails stuck in the mud by the riverbank, swaying in the wind, not going anywhere. He'd grown up somewhere down there. His memory flooded with thoughts deep and murky, filled with strange debris, bumping in the currents. The river pushed against the banks and the cattails swayed and the mud pushed back.

They said doing time was like a river. But a river didn't have to worry about crossing state lines and breaking parole. A river didn't have to be back at work on Monday morning or stand losing a job. A river didn't have to pay rent by the end of the month or stand getting evicted. The river just flowed, and where it stopped flowing, it disappeared in the ocean. Paying for the past was nothing like a river.

At the end of the bridge they took an exit ramp, turning around just short of a full circle. From there the road extended under the bridge and went south. They followed the road until they came to a gas station where they pulled over. Four clowns sitting in a van looked back at Emmett in the convenient store window.

Lou opened the door. "I'm sick of driving," he said. "Somebody filler up and somebody take the wheel. Oh, and don't forget to spring a leak before we leave."

"We're fresh out of cash. Should we tip the police off before or after we loot the place?" Glen asked.

"We aren't no hobos," Charles said. "But I sure could use a bite to eat."

"Speak for yourself." Emmett said and spat out the window.

Glen squinted one eye. "Do you think she'll follow us this far?"

A fly bumped against the back window. Nobody moved. "She will," Lou said.

"Maybe we should wait for her. Say what you've got to say and walk away," Charles said.

"Won't make no difference," Emmett said. "Obviously she's upset."

Lou stuck his hands in his back pockets. "Have it your way."

Emmett eyed two dogs out in the field chasing their shadows. For a moment there he thought they'd take flight and disappear in the sun. Doing time was more like the wind than a river. It could be felt, but not seen. Even after you got out, the pressure was always there, the clock ticking down the moments of your freedom, the feeling like you might have to go back.

"Sometimes when you're out on the road, you don't know where you're going," he said.

Lou shrugged his shoulders and left in search of a bathroom.

A breeze passed through the space between the windows. Charles climbed out the side. "Going for a stroll," he said. He looked back, winked, and was gone.

Glen followed him out and grabbed the pump. He stuck the nozzle in the side and watched as the numbers ticked away.

Emmett eyed the driver's seat but didn't budge. He wondered what he was going to say when she caught up to them. He heard a knuckle knocking the glass behind him.

Glen passed him a credit card through a slit in the side window. "Don't tell the others."

Emmett read the name on the card. Sarah Little. Glen's wife. He'd have to forge her signature. He went inside the store and grabbed enough sandwiches and beer to carry them through the day.

A man in a white T-shirt and cut-off shorts glanced up from behind the cash register. He had on a baseball cap flipped around backward, and a hand on the counter pawing a sports magazine.

"Gas. Pump 2," Emmett said, pointing at the van.

The clerk looked out the window in a slow sort of way. Emmett followed his eyes there. The station only had two pumps, one which was unoccupied.

The clerk pushed a button on the register and handed Emmett a receipt. Emmett signed it in a loose-handed style and returned it. He wondered how he'd ever started down this road, this life of crime. The clerk compared the signatures and gave him back the card.

"My wife," Emmett lied. "She don't mind."

"Are you guys from the circus?"

Emmett pulled the red balloon off his nose and stuck it on the counter. "Birthday party. But if anyone asks, we're from the university. Professors. Got it?"

"What?"

"You got a girlfriend?"

"No."

"Why not?"

"We broke up."

Emmett paused. "Who broke it off, you or her?"

"She did."

"And did you try to get her back?"

"Yeah." The clerk looked down at the counter and flipped a page.

"And did that work out?"

"No."

"Why not?"

"She said I was stalking her. Said she'd call the police."

The clerk tapped a photo stuck under the glass. Emmett leaned over and took a closer look.

"Beautiful," he said.

The clerk didn't reply.

"My wife, you see, she's a little confused right now. If she stops in here, tell her it wasn't us. You didn't see four guys in clown suits. We're just old friends from the university going down to the river to catch some fish."

"Sure," the clerk said and scratched his baseball cap. "But why do you have her credit card? You said she doesn't mind."

"Oh, whatever." Emmett swung the door all the way open on the way out.

"I might need to see some ID before you start chugging down those beers." The clerk's voice came out muffled behind the glass.

Emmett kept walking.

Glen took up the driver's seat. Lou sat in the back. Charles showed up a minute later. He smelled like cut grass. He climbed in and sat down next to Lou. Lou took one look at him, threw his hand up in the air, and shook his head.

Emmett jumped in the passenger seat up front and shut the door. "Let's go," he said.

Half an hour down the road, Charles dropped something out the side of his mouth. Lou caught it in the wind. "The math's gotta add up."

"Don't stir up the bee's nest," Lou mumbled.

Glen kept his eyes fixed on the road, two hands on the wheel. He leaned forward. "Find some music. I'm falling asleep."

Emmett watched the river go by, and the road, and the shadows encroaching on the land stuck between the two. The road darkened and the shadows danced in and out of the water. He flipped on the radio and listened to the static. He saw no reason to change the station. Glen finally reached over and turned it off.

"The turn-off should be just up ahead," Lou said.

Emmett looked in the mirror and watched the moonlight on the faces behind him, clowns in the near dark. He felt like he'd aged a hundred years in a just one night and didn't know why. The light changed from pale white to red and blue.

"Fuck." Glen slowed the van and pulled it over. "The Man."

The Man turned out to be a woman. She flooded a wide-beam flashlight onto their faces, pausing at each one, slow as a boat churning ice mid-winter. Glen handed her his driver's license.

"Are you clowns from the circus?" she asked.

Glen sighed. "Birthday party, officer. It's a long story."

"I've got time. Spill it. And wash that makeup off your face. I need to get a clear ID."

Emmett pulled a towel out of a bag at his feet and handed it to Glen.

"We're going fishing, ma'am," Lou said, leaning forward. "But Emmett here, his wife is dead set against it. We did his grandson's birthday party and then high-tailed it out of there before she had a chance to suss out what was what. Do you intend to report us, ma'am?"

"What difference does that make?"

"She'll find us. She will."

"How's that? She a cop?"

"Parole officer. She's got friends. They'll help her."

"Do you know why I pulled you over?"

"You know her too?" Glen asked.

"You've got out-of-state plates. Routine inspection. There's nothing to report here. Not unless one of you is breaking parole."

"I signed his wife's name on a credit card back at the gas station. Is that going to be a problem?" Emmett asked.

Lou tagged him on the head from behind. "Now we're dead."

The officer eyed the exterior of the van, waving the short end of the driver's license in her face as if it might cool her down in the summer night heat. "I think you've got bigger problems than me."

"How's that, ma'am?"

"Credit cards are easy to track. Any half-rate PI could find you in a heartbeat."

"That true?"

"I think I'm just going to let you boys ramble on down the road. Expect to be on her radar early tomorrow, if she's serious about finding you."

Glenn put the towel down on the dashboard. The rainbow of makeup smeared across his face made him less identifiable than ever. He smiled a big yellow-toothed smile out the window. "Thank you, officer."

She warped her lips to the side and stared at him. His nose matched the nose of nobody in particular. He took the license from her extended hand. She flipped her hat back and pulled it down on her head with both hands. Glen held on to his fake smile.

"You're free to go," she said and waved her arm down the road. "Just watch your speed in this county."

"Aren't you going to search us?" Charles called from the back.

"I might have some narcotics in my shorts."

"Knock it off," Lou said, waving a fist in his direction.

She narrowed her gaze. "The way I figure it, you're all too old to be running from the law."

"How do you know we're old, ma'am?" Lou asked.

"Honey, I can tell you're old just by the way you talk."

Charles snickered. "If you're looking for honey, I'm your lucky charm."

Lou tagged him on the shoulder and Charles took a swat back at him, soft as a fly-swatter.

"If you haven't noticed," Glen mentioned under his breath, leaning out the window, "he's single."

"He's not exactly my type," she said in a raspy whisper, somewhat louder than she'd been talking.

"Thank you again, ma'am," Lou said. "We've got a long drive ahead. If you don't mind, we'll be on our way."

They found the turn-off ten minutes later. The warehouse was dark. Emmett tried the door, but it was chain shut from the outside. He broke the lock off with a rock and went inside and pulled the front gate open. Glen eased the van inside and stopped a few feet from the gate. He cut the engine and Emmett lowered the gate as the fumes dispersed.

Upstairs they found a room with four cots, dust for bed covers. Lou took the shower before anyone could object. Glen pulled off his clown suit and dropped it on the floor and sat down on a cot. He leaned over and fell asleep, in shorts and socks, his feet still on the ground. Emmett looked out the second floor window for traffic but the road remained dead in the night.

He thought he heard a train whistle blowing out across the fields, miles away and powering onward to nowhere. Or maybe it was the sound of the wind rushing through a window left open in the middle of a storm. It reminded him of his childhood, a time when he was unable to sleep because he felt the seasons changing. The feeling stayed with him and carried over into his dreams.

In the morning they gathered around a crate in the middle of the warehouse floor. Lou brought out crowbars and cutters from a bag and they took to prying off wooden planks and snipping bands from the pallet. Glen wheeled a crane over and wrapped a chain around the large metallic box in the middle of all the lose boards. He hoisted the safe up in the air and spun it around a time and stopped it with the door facing them. They helped him cleared the floor below.

Charles opened his bag and pulled out some tools. He looked at the safe and picked up a hammer and chisel. "This may take a while," he said.

Lou went off to make coffee and Glen assembled the fishing poles. The sun headed for the peak of the sky. Emmett wondered why he ran from Kelly, why he didn't just put his foot down. "You only get one chance with that woman," he muttered, but nobody heard him. He let his head drop and he dozed off.

Some time later his thoughts cleared again. He sat there fidgeting, watching Charles play with the lock. The king of clowns had been at the safe for a while now and couldn't get it to budge. They had no idea what was inside, but the safe weighed more than it should have, according to the specs. It weighed a million dollars more.

Charles hoisted the safe up higher by the chain and pushed it around so he could get a better look at it in a different light. Emmett wheeled his chair across the cement floor to keep an eye on the door. He didn't want Charles getting his hands on the loot before they had a chance to count it.

Charles continued working, slowly, methodically, fruitlessly. The clock was tick-tocking and they weren't getting any richer. Emmett sighed.

"Let's get a drink," Glen said.

Charles ignored him.

"Char, come on. Give that thing a break. It'll still be here when we get back."

Charles took a look at his watch before he put his tools down. "OK."

They got good and stinking drunk in town. Years rolled off Charlie's face. Before long they were laughing loud enough to get noticed. Nobody in the bar seemed to care. Emmett felt a chill run over him and stopped drinking long enough to look out the window. Cars were passing by in slow cadence, caught in the rhythm of the mid-day traffic.

"Couldn't we get inside the safe without popping the lock?" Glen asked.

Charles eyeballed him, trying to make out the logic, and then the clouds cleared. He laughed so hard he pissed himself. Glen's beer leaned over at a precarious angle and spilled on the table, and his leg, and the floor. Lou jumped up and backed away. Emmett pulled his beer off the table before it was too late. Charles looked up like he was going to apologize, and then he lost it again, giggling until he went over the edge. They waited for him to get back up and calm down.

He turned his head to the side and laid it on the table. "I think I hear a train a coming."

When they got back to the warehouse the safe was open. And empty. Lou was furious. He grabbed Charles by the shoulders and stuffed his head in the safe. "How come you can't open it and someone else can?"

"Back off," Glen said, a crowbar in hand. Lou took a step back and Charles straightened up.

"So what happened, Char?" Emmett asked, after Glen put the crowbar down.

Charles inspected the lock on the safe. It hadn't been touched. He looked inside with a flashlight. A black gadget stuck to the wall. He pulled it out.

"Timer," he said. "I had no idea."

Lou squinted before speaking. "What did we lose?"

Charles sniffed the air and stuck his head back inside. "Chemicals," he said, his voice muffled.

He came out of the safe and sighed. "I'll analyze the residue."

"We better do some fishing. Or this whole trip is going to be a waste," Emmett said.

In the afternoon, Kelly found him stuck in the cattails down by the riverside.

"Why do you always run from me?" she asked.

"I don't know. Just to see if you'll follow."

They sat down in the weeds where the earth was dry, up and away from the lap of the water. The river continued to bump against the mud and the mud pushed back.

"You remember that first day we met, back in high school?" she asked.

"I remember a time you punched me in the nose. Is that the day you're talking about?"

"I said I'd never give up on you."

"I know."

"I got your money."

"What?"

"When I found the warehouse, and nobody was there, I didn't know what was going on. Then the safe clicked and I opened it."

"No drugs?"

"Stacks of 100s wrapped in paper. And a bag of coke. I spilled it in the river."

He looked down at the water and wondered where the powder had gone. After all, time was like a river. "What do you want to do now?"

"Should we tell the others?"

"No, let's let them think you're still angry at me," he said.

"Why would they think that?"

"No reason."

She shook her head. "After all these years, there's one thing you've never understood about me."

"What's that?"

"I like fishing, too."

"Well," he said. "Why didn't you want me to go?"

"I know those other clowns you run around with. They're never up to anything good."

"I guess I should have invited you then."

The wind paused and the cattails dipped a little closer to the water.

"I see you got a catfish in that bucket over there." She waved at the mud. The river had almost pushed the bucket over.

"Sure enough, I do."

"Let's go tell the others."

"About the fish? Or the money?"

"About our trip to Mexico."

"We're going to Mexico?"

"We got to spend all that money somewhere."

He pecked her on the cheek and said, "Yeah, I guess we do."

When they got back to the warehouse, the van was gone. Kelly's car was parked in the tall grass nearby. They found a note stuck to the window.

Gone to join the circus.

Clowns on the Run

As he climbed in the car, Emmett heard a freight train in the distance, barreling down on thin tracks, a long way to go before it reached home. Mexico sounded like a good place. It was as good a place as any for a pair of clowns on the run.

Daniel Scott White runs the award winning Longshot Press, known for publishing short works by great authors such as Martha Wells, Ken Liu, Yoon Ha Lee, Emily Devenport, and more. He studied the music business at Columbia College in Chicago and went on to assist in the recording of a project for Bob Dylan. Along with earning an MBA degree, he worked for an international publisher focusing on children's books and textbooks. While his expertise is in business, his passion is in writing. He was born in the mountains but now lives by the sea.

Please consider leaving an honest review

Reviews are vital for readers and authors. Every review that readers leave helps hundreds of other people find new books to love. And it can make or break a book.

So, if you enjoyed this book, please write an honest review on the site where you found it. Reviews mean more readers, and more readers mean that I can publish more books featuring great stories by talented authors.